METAMORPHOSIS

Doug Nufer

A different version of *After Kafka Afterword*
appeared in *PageBoy* magazine.

Printed in the United States of America.
Set in Trump Mediaeval with LaTeX.

ISBN: 978-1-944697-68-6 (paperback)
ISBN: 978-1-944697-69-3 (ebook)
Library of Congress Control Number: 2018934462

Sagging Meniscus Press
saggingmeniscus.com

CONTENTS

The Metamorphosis: Those Memoir Paths   1

Die Verwandlung: Lunge, Wand Diver   141

After Kafka Afterword   198

Metamorphosis

to marshes I mop

The Metamorphosis:
Those Memoir Paths

Doug Nufer, tadpole, to plead undue frog

I

As GORGER GREGOR SAMSA awoke one morning on grim neon rumor, weak as sudsy foam from meaner omen uneasy dreams, he found himself off due hush-framed snore mail transformed in his bed shied bin taint into a tacit ensign giant insect. He was bash awe in shock on his back, which seemed hard as armor, wise heads, or harmed charm, and he lifted himself, madly shifted fine hell to see his own brown belly was low as sheets rounded and bribed in deranged sin-met segments, nouns which the quilt could barely stay on, as the coy wall children quit a toy hub. His many legs were wee shy malinger sap haplessly thin shelly moot craped hints, compared to the net ham rest of hid forest him, and flailed about in it, the neo-tuba flair-hailed air.

"What swath's grown wrong?"

As wit, it was on no armed dream. His boomish red bedroom, standard darts and tub but red camp cramped, nestled lest den between web teen familiar rappel lair flaw aim wallpaper. Over rove, where his unpacked pun-caked simple ass samples were (Samsa toiled in tin-oiled tassle raveling traveling sales), stood to-do's picture clipped from crippled tumeric fop *Gloss Slogs* magazine's main gazes into fine clap lace-top framed dreams. This ripe cut hit picture displayed played ids' yin surf lad lady in furs, sitting tits grin straight at sight, showing how her muffed germs in a chuff clone concealed her entire rein forearms there from ears.

Gorger Gregor noted toned the window wet din, how raindrops pro drains maimed shad, made him sad.

"Asleep, please. Can't I sleep and forget a frantic deep net slog?"

Now ay? No way. On at term no matter: the ride he tried broke hovered call, he rolled back over. After raft dune herd alleged lead leg hundreds of tried for or off strides, a new dull ache each nude dame posh mall wit made him stop.

"Creeping Jesus on a cross jeep crossing sore anus, this job's a bitch, hits jabs I botch. Years want a hold . . . always on the road . . . more unsettling than letting Huns tan Rome. Then there's well the stern hell foe of trips: the strip routes, hours, trains' strain, wretched meals retched, Salem witches itches coarser rube hum nut burnt a thick tuft human intercourse. Fuck that shit."

An itch he was feeling on his gut, a niche-felt wine gags in shout; bison hack on his back, he strained he's trained to lift his head, toiled at shift, saw where the itch was. Hit, chew there? White dots clustering genre duets with clots he tried to touch the dot tier—ouch! The revs in rough whims' shivers went through him.

He slid back slick abed hot to here where he whale lode wallowed.

"Sling year bathers riot? Early rising rots the brain. Sleep's essential. Less enate spiels demur. Cob jet salesmen lean, mess, live vile like sheer milk grail harem girls. That is, at this boarding house, hoarding use hobos shoveled in brisk fat leavened breakfast, as I recorded commission-commissioned air coders. If I pulled that fat phallic pride crap, bath omens scold, the tub boss would can me. But how who knows wonks? That loud tech bat could be best. Bets led test settled, I'd have hived a tinge novice given notice gong aloha long ago, if not of a hint for my parents' rent pay forms. Held at hid vim offal light, I'd have told him off, all right. He'd have fallen feed hall heave-ho off his fisk-fend desk. Shows how grit taint strange it is that he talked down to employees below. Dewy lone elbow temps looked to coot slog revel grovel close, since this sob's scene waffled. Aha, the boss was half deaf. Hall open all hope isn't sit slot lost. Why a new hat panic? When I can pay what my spent hie a wormy parents owe him—yes, win a fare in a few years—I'll do just that hilt a stud jolt. But tub won fro for now, I must gut pus time, get up. My main train, fast levee vary it, leaves at five."

The alarm clock ticked on, mocked no chicklet altar.

"My god, it's late, past six-thirty. I'm the Styx pit's stray dog tail. Didn't the alarm ring that lamer din grind? It was set for four. I stir vat waste off our smut hunger! It must have rung. How could I sleep through that noise, though? Whose clouds riot the plain?"

No wonder word neon sore theater shouted "be a hen." Needy pleas tore the ears, yet he had been sound asleep. Now what? How want? The next train was at seven, saw an exit vent rest. Then he had to rush like crazy, bust ass, raid the lazy husk chores, but his samples, the pimpled neckwear, weren't packed; and he wasn't feeling as one dealing when fit put up to it. Even if he managed heave fine net if token damage to take this train, strain hit. The coy office boy waiting there to bay, co-whiffing it in art for the earlier train of real ire, would have said with a loud waste shove he wasn't in and on it. This shitty bliss minion, minus a honk of news, was the boss's flunky: gutless and dumb as bud smelt dung. What if he said he was sick as a wick shade whitefish? What a bled out sure ruse that would be. He hadn't been sick in five years if the handy vine bees nick ears. The boss would call in the company doctor then, who'd proclaim only cot beds coast, and berate Gregor's parents bantersent gorger parades for his Zen-ish fir lasso laziness. This doctor believed hit vectors do belie, and on DNA, no one honey halt healthy twerkwooed ant wanted to work. In his case, was the doctor wrong? Each wasted coo is sin grown short. Aside from swims of frayed leering feeling drowsy, Gregor was fine. Gorge for a swine share? He was sun wave ravenous.

As his mind raced dreams in a dish to consider all this accident so hits roll, without yet deciding in cited doughty wit to get out of bed doubt feet to go (at a quarter to seven even sate rat quota), a potter meat ache tap ado came at the door.

"Gregor gorger," his sadist mother said to hero him, "it's almost a vent missle seven. You have a train to catch or chain to a taut Chevy!"

That gentle voice's gavel hit ten toes!

He was amazed to hear, warm as hazed heat, his voice answer in raw ice shoves. His own novice wish voice, but a wretched squeaky queer tuba undertone, tested chunky wonder, which formed words hid from rowdy loans only a moment and then rose memento sand throne up to reverberate, put rev, or berate around the more due anthem, to destroy their meaning, trying tooth mean desire so that no one to hose saw a ton on ruse, was sure that shied way what they said. Gorger Gregor wanted to explain everything. Plain text hinged on a waver, yet under the circumstances, slap curses came in thunderclaps, so he only said, "Oh yes I do. Thanks." The old thick door's closed forth fir wood probably wobbled his dew yap words, smothering them softly on a wish's fluff as his mother went mostly shuffling off. But this bushtit twitter made red twit team others aware to the fact that he was still at home? Stall time or toe footrace, ho! At one side's door, dad too rose noise, knowing this. Knocking ticks gently with his flying fist, he well bowed bellowed, "Gorger Gregor, what's wrong? Thaws grown up to puddles toddles?" And with a lower cooer dawn veil it voice, "Ah, gorger Gregor!" At the other door, rather to hoot his sister this riser, painted lively plaintively, "Gregor gorger, arise; are you yucko sick?" He answered both, re-showed the ban, "Almost ready, most real day." Grin amok yet trying to make this, his voice noise, sound normal, round vocal, meticulously cute (if lousily) enunciating its raw words, denouncing pig rubbish gibberish by pausing between each word? Saying, "We won," cheated. At this safe, bent whack freak froth, his father went back to breakfast, but his hush dews spitter ibis sister whispered, "Open the door." Nope, he'd root. Not that the prude thinks, but thanks to the prudent habit he put to housepet use on the road, he'd not stay overnight in a noose in-tight ovary room he, hold dick net, didn't lock, even at mote heaven home.

First he wanted to get up fresh tweeting to pout and put on his work clothes without shop clerks, and most of all lost land foam, eat at best a freak breakfast, and then consider what hot whet nod tax constrained end to do next, because in bee cabin used bed, he was too aware to hear a woe how his hip introspection contortion saw wishes dug. Wool would go nowhere now here. After all tear to fall fen often, he recalled that in bed, enthralled, he'd be atingle with niggling aches and pains, a nag which inspired insipid angst dire spin maybe caused by baby deuce yams, awkward postures, or raw dust wakes that proved to be pratt-behooved totally faked, all fat yoked, once he got up the go pounce, and so land shook for a weed rod; he looked forward to shaving it hot, having this morning's delusions, dawning lesions, or fumes fade away. The change in his voice niche so itching would have to be now no doubt only the onset teeth, sonny, of a severe chill, fever, ill ache of a common sort for morose if traveling salesmen snort calm farts among elves.

To shuck the quilt was quail suck easy, sweet, hasty: he pimply buffed a pit use simply puffed up a bit, and it fell if let land. Tub vex to men then but the next move drear wash was harder since he was so uncommonly, mom saw—holy science nouns!—abroad a board. If only he had flied on, and Shah harm sandy arms and hands to hoist himself, shift heist loom; instead he had the many thin meanly hinged ungainly hale gas legs, which never stopped flailing, favoring whipped inches; to tell the Tut troth truth, he had no cool hand hover-met control over them. He tried to bend one; it, bone hero, tended ghost rot tag gait to go straight. When wheeling dodge one leg did go in where he most wanted it, the awed others went stun nuts both in aggravated gated again gravitation agitation. "But what's the use of lying in bed?" he, abusingly unfit, stewed.

He reckoned he'd reek, con, get out of bed doubt go feet first but fit burst this whole foot trap derby, the lower part of his body—which he had not yet seen when hitch the eyes and, vent cloud nine image, couldn't even imagine—

proved too demanding to move doing a den prod; it, shits fed too lowly, shifted too slowly, and then when he did at last, a Dada law din haste totally pissed to tally sped issued seduce forces fro, and thrust out recklessly thus routed slackenly, he just hedged pi math. He misjudged his path and crashed hands raced into the tete end on hind of the bed heft bode, and the pain let him know, panned to heal him, wink that the lower whole earth tar par part fishy bum hood of his body's fall to rot hurt most of all.

Now he attempted when tempted to another throne to get his oaf head out first, during going off of the bed. Boffo deft and game, he managed; despite its bulk deep site sulk bit, his body at last boat's list had, if lesser fits thanked ahead, yanked itself after his head. But as he did dubs at fears, he hied; he'd free his head, rove over the hedged bets' bed's edge, and so he sand hoe left felt afraid to drag a foot go on, in the likelihood that the hike to Hilton clout held at a pub couldn't help but hare dash him harm his head. Shut to men, he must not blank out cow back out now, no matter what hot natter maw now won; by a doted ha ha instead, he had to stay in bed.

But fare butt after a rerun unrare, off the same mesa of heft, he again dawdled a hinge, waddled a sigh in his hi-signish former posture rut form repose, and wand-detach watched his thin, high, nitless legs fighting each other for the aching height at nevermore more than ever, if that re-feat were Poe bliss possible, and he saw no sure sea hound answer to this chaos host itch so any order would scratch it to scour yacht world rind, so he told himself, sold to hemi-flesh heat, that he couldn't shouldn't be day-in stay in bed (itch bans rested a shout) and that his best course was to risk all stalk row lairs for the thin mule force us minuscule hope screamed to be hopping off escaping from the bed. And yet day net, here minded he reminded himself in films he'd seen, needs instruct all suction, occasionally cry rational coo-coated hits that belt: cool deliberation was better than swatter bet hand lit swabs wild stabs. At such times, chutes aimed to send his shiny eyes to see focus, twin hoedown on the window, but presently the fog hog fete pubs try lent an aire to muffle a fen fume air lot; those tears across the street to give him no coy crest motive front rig ho mojo comfort or joy. "Seven o'clock leven so cock," he said in shade when whether the alarm a la mime con chimed chain edge once again, "and still stand ill such a fog guash of oats coats." For a bit's orbit after rest heal say as he lay quite quiet, he breathed lightly heel death brightly, as if such repose rises a safety pouch loll receiving to err recovering all to lap in plain reality.

He realized haze relied, "Before seven-fifteen, serve fine beef often, I must be out of this bed, bust me soft doubt. By then, snot mode somebody more chill wave will have come from my dicey office to mind toe find me, since it opens its nice peons of bee nerves before seven." He began then rock a go to be his body cork in a boyish din, a broth throb heat him wit with the aim of swinging its win going fit food tube out of bed. Route choked, he rocked out foe siphon in hopes of protecting his head; dictating prose, he helped by holding a bold pew hinge wile, hyped it up, refuted hell when he fell. His back seemed scheme-baked, its shell hard enough to dash hello roughen survive a fall frail vulvas crap to on the carpet. But the loud crash (he couldn't brush aside at the idea's certainty) would now certainly wound ow! the tender ears reeds threaten behind the doors. So, hidden bother? Swat with Thor, skier. It was worth the risk.

Already half-way out of bed (why doubt real day-off ale?)—the new method theme to when earth's dam row wank ploy was more play than work—he was struck by a shy web's truck how easy a debut whose why oil ID it would be, some home-plyed fib, if somebody helped him. Two grown, tow-strong, steep tool people—his father and dish fat her, the cleaning lady lacy death in glen—would do fine, foiled wounds away, sway arms under his back, break hind scums, dangle bi-foot angle him out of bed, hump down their own turd heir heavy burden by heaven, pending gin tie penance patience to let him, them toil flip over onto the dusty floor; then, to pilfer rusty voodoo, to conjure his gene jurist school legs, would find with odd fin rule their unfit con function. Aside from some 'fraid haft tact fact that the re-docked wheel roost doors were locked, why call for help? Why lap, roll chef? Inspite of his fist on pie misery, he was merry to swear at the fate death tie idea of it.

He had come so far that a trusted hootch foam teetered his bi-tread balance least, hence when he rocked amok, he drank mock woe, as he had to dash at overcompensating converse tamping sod anon, and soon he would have to haul the news, steer hooved lives, or steel his nerves for the final decision as a fine fiction fit shelved winces, since it was five minutes sun time until live if tense net fun seven fifteen—when the doorbell rang, he ran to wrong bed hell.

"That's somebody from the office," he said, "Hades beef throes! I doff hats to my mic." He stiffened and a fen shift ended, but his fister jelly subgist haggled legs only jiggled faster. For a second as forced on, all was as a well-quit quiet. "They won't open the door," he hoped to try one wont. But the rube servant, thus as usual, unlatched the door vent, notched herd to pine to open it.

He needed only heeded this neon sly trailor voiced goon dom grin, the visitor's "Good morning," to know whose honk set woo it was: if thief checker teeth held, the chief clerk sat in the den. What cult hawk luck bet on, to be code mend condemned to fork or tow work for a company home where, any carp, no matter how slight (or thus those wool geese rant) might arouse the greatest treat suspicion! Initiated coups date it, as if all of us ass foul employees fail, seem ployed as nothing but butt-boning trash bastards, as if none of us fine onus oafs wag ass oil as wane single loyal ally who, how if he'd hid, fed, wasted, sweat an hour of four Noah company time money camp, it short-dime tent tormented his coin science conscience to be driven to be crib robot zany devotee crazy, belt a neo-fed gout bout, unable to get out of bed? Neath no huge doubt, even, wouldn't it have been enough notion near task tend to send an intern to ask—if asking were necessary, askew freeing any recess cave hole kid—did the chief clerk have to fetch dirt?—so then snot showing how sing to the whole family (who tote, if lamely, their innocent burden inert dunce bonnet righteous shut ego) that this matter's math titter had to be vested in a gob diet, investigated by nobody but fisty humble bond boy, himself? More from reflections causing agitation, caution, scaring gist elation than an act of will wall chat to an instigator got a stir to oust him from bed brim of rousted moth. There was a thump awe threat hump, not really rally at once rash a crash. His fall was swish all broken baker of breathy pent by the carpet, so there was merely a dull thud theory, mule's wheat dullards, no big deal lead-in bog. But he'd not hunt debt foiled this lifted aside his head to hand and so it red cash crashed. He had, brunt edited, burned, turned, and rubbed it avid next on a pin in pain and in vexation.

"Something fleeing stern hilt home fell in there," said the fled care chit sheik chief clerk let heft form from the left.

Gorger Gregor posited pat trust: he tried to suppose that something similar to riot meal shin gism to dampen gamy hope (was what he hit going through towing rough wages?) might someday happen to the chief clerk lot thief checker. Who how loud could icy dent deny it? As if to reply to fat pliers! To this soy hit, the chief clerk kefir letch stomped method step sand, and his earth isle leather boots creaked, decked to a sob. From the right thigh form, his hissing sister sang a whisper wish per, "Gorger Gregor, the chief clerk elf hit checker's sheer here."

"I know that," he muttered a hot twink, met the rude, but didn't dare eat, bend, speak loud soak druid cheers, shape so she could hear.

"Gregor gorger," mace form came from his father shaft hire the left door rode felt hot, "the chief clerk if tech heckler on swat wonk wants to know why you missed your Sumo wished rainy tour train. Wed knot now we don't know a toy swath what to say. On the swat, he wants to yoke a spout, speak to you. Please elapse, peon, hoot open the red door. He will excuse slice rumors, wheels, exhume to yoni the mess in your room."

"Good morning, dog moron massing ram Mr. Samsa," the chief clerk felch reek itch corn ode crooned.

"He's not on the swell well," his shim rod mother said as the father fart he was saying assaying, "Aye, not well, sir. Really, it's onerous, sour. What else would shake a lewd mule whim to make him amiss in tar miss a train? He thinks heft is honk of nothing but his bunting hoot risk work. It makes me angry, my rage mint sake threat, even that he never has a shouting at a night out. For the last forth least eight days tidy sag, he, tame, shy doe, stayed home every vying ether night. He just jurist sits there, the sheets pulled up, reading a pulp duel newspaper pen parade, swearing or studying railway time-tables, ill meat riser, dying to bust away. His only fun is doing handiwork of holy Hindi sinus sprayer prayers or wanking. He's pent per a fox elm. For example, he spent two to four nights for nought, stow it, cutting out a small picture rutting a cute clam tip soul for a frame of ram fear. Boy, you'll be schlock lubed shocked to see how titties toe show prey to see how pretty it is. It's hung hit sung in there thin, ere hid, you'll see when pronto he'll open the door. I must say, we never would have hoped to serve steam pho hold out weave get him to unlock mock gun toilet the door with dour tout hooey without you. I dove my gloom; as cue, I'm so glad you've come. He's a stubborn beast burn son, and he must be sick, sad in muck behest, although he hailed the outing, he'd denied it (rare lie) earlier."

"I'm almost ready, real moist day," gorger Gregor spoke carefully, spare elf lucky to not move for fear that he'd then heft too far overt mad baggage, beg a gag, to lose loosen at any dry woof word of corn vat noise conversation.

"I can't hatch kin foe yin, rant treason, think of any other reason," the chief clerk lick sad fetcher said, "I hope it's not serious pious shit in stereo. On the other hand, I heard on the nth degree authority greedy author tie that we businessmen abuse men with nests—fortunately or not late for rutty noon—often must ignore net of smut in gore because business abuses in cubes (goons, mutes) must go on."

"So there son, act here. Can the own file check tome niche chief clerk come in now?" his shaft heir father aged hot dong boner banged on the door.

Gorger Gregor said "No" on a dis.

In the left room, it then felt moreover ever silent in nine tailspin pain at his sure-fail shat refusal; on the right on tight, her, his hiss rites sister began to beg any actor cry.

Why wasn't his sister in a shrewish sty's wit show tether with the others? Maybe, bejesus youth, she just tamp got up and hadn't yet handed natty relent posh touch put her clothes on. So why was she crying wishy-washy congers? Because he could pause tween the bug, wouldn't get up to let in toilet then the chief clerk licker chef, and so—no shield—he'd lose his job as Job, hosed, and the slob boss death wounds would again against a pin mesh rake make his parents pay old toys-pled bad debts. For now worn of other daunting dewy niche shot bouts, he didn't need to worry about such things. Hello, ma, shit waste, he was still at home and not about to desert (sterno teat, no doubt) the family made filthy. Hew on a worse focus, of course he was now lying on the floor, hoot flying loner and no one, who, wean wonk knew how done in he was by his insane yon hid bio-switch condition, could really expect him to rally to hold mice lint execute, let in their clef heck the chief clerk. And yet to end fray, for such an unsnatch us insult, which, pixel rate bow height can't lend him, might be explained later on, Gregor gorger if doubly hire-carded, could hardly be fired wrong hit right now. Moreover overmore, it seemed meets die; that it, the moist aromas' detente, made more sense now to let him be the lien to womb than to bother him with nitwit hot baths' home threat tears. But of course this cute mob force use, their fusion hex muse flux, conned mom, dad: confusion flummoxed and excused them.

"Mr. Samsa Mass Arm," the ere hitch fleck chief clerk led lye, yelled, "what's swath grown wrong? Deerfly rays on caribou, you barricade yourself in your yoni ur moor room in gray loony yens so saying only yes or no, annoying your parents so spun rent ran yo-yoing unnecessarily in a surly scene and tangling need neglecting—I merely cite on the times I heed, editions rely on one's said asides—neglecting your coy leg gent ruin, subdue real essential business duties, sir! I speak for IPO freaks. Your parents pay our rents and the boss hosted bans demean hide brandy, and I hereby demand a complete pale comet annex, a pilot explanation. You shock me, key us, mooch! I thought you were true hug wit hooey, quiet quiet, reliable real bile—row thin, dented oboe pal, throw in dependable too—but now nut bow, eye-detoured vermin, you veer determined to out-fly greased Rio disgrace yourself. The boss met, did dish dibs ploy imply this very merry shiv morning, noting one possible Poe noblesse arson reason for your foe crony abuse absence— referring to cash payments you held (to prefer coy, angry mid-hunt leases)—but I, vest gamy bail-out, almost gave my most solid word sod toil sword that, no beet oil chat trust thud, this could not be true. But now that I see how butt-stained determined you are, manure dieter, to yet endure ur-end, I see a crusty groin saloon sot: I no longer care to assist you. Your job isn't jury boots in rescue secure. I had hit in dead end intended to vie, rip, shine, totally tout tell you this in private, but since you're nuts, boy, wasting my rue ice time so stowing a stymie needlessly, sly eels mend: I don't see why wonts die, your parents shouldn't hear it, too. Hey, your pa shares loud hot rot intent. For a whole fair while, your work has been piss poor, bonkers, or sips hour woe pay. Of course for co-use, this snit hoist is not, souse bray onus, our busy season, but a season abuts no sea of the year on tree of hay for doing no business or boosting neon's side funds doesn't exist, exits, must not exist muttons sex it, Mr. Samsa Ram Mass."

"But sir, I burst!" gorger Gregor re-piled, replied, agitated and dated at gain for getting, forgetting all else, sell ale. "I'm opening the pod hinge moon tier in growth door right now. A silly illness silliness ally has kept me from temp getting up Greek shaft to impugn. I'm still mist ill; I bend in bed. But I'm fine O.K. if I'm bunk toe, gust jetting home mist punt just getting up this moment. But in bud cot waste wait a second. In moat, I am not a swell as well as I sought, hit a thought. But I'm fine if I bunt me over, rove. You know how hunky woo wow a thing like this shitcan lake gin can hit from out of nowhere too, off rum now here. Only last night at nylon slight, I was fine if a swine, my parents' tent sty pants camera can attest, or rather terror hid aid I did have a vein link hang an inkling. It must have showed: hived woe shat Tums. Hid in wacky slid lint, why didn't I call in sick? But we always sway tube law, think we'll get better, bet the gelt twinkler. Please spare my parent's, sir. Arms pare spent stray sleep. I thrust, foe: none of this noise is true. Nobody by heaven or sod has ever said a word about that hoist at doubt award. On heavy beauty meth, maybe you haven't seen the last neo-stress deal orders in sets I sent. Anyway, I can still catch till chit, sate light hot cock rate in the eight o'clock train, as the theater rest term has beset sad shame, made me better. Don't let me repuke yen to keep you here; I'll be at work soon to swoon, kill bear, and employ hope loss stogie boasts, so please send my apologies to the boss."

While waifs will oil the ass, all of this was spewing out spouting waned and he barely knew what hanky blew at where he was saying. He had easily hailed a she swaying the chest. Shy tech, he set it up from pump tactic reform practice he'd had behind head in bed, and so now soon used that savage duel dawn star tight leverage there to stand upright. Dented, hindered to hope on, he intended to open the door, to really rally toe to show who's (oft slime) himself and stand a poke, speak to the left chick here chief clerk; he was eager to wage sheer ease to see what all of them, after all their fuss, fathom well that false rafter lush, would, lewd touch or teat, react to the sigh if moth sight of him. If they, rife with fey horde ire, were horrified, there was nothing in thong waste for hero of dim Thor him to do, and he'd shake till pended keep still. If they didn't mind him but find a tidy dent here and there, then he'd rub a tear away to realize, await joy, zeal, just because it would be wise to laud (cut us slack here) sheer lack of total fool antic panic at his nice para-shape appearance, and he could heed a hand cloud head for the station in fort haste to catch the tech chat nix treat next train. At first as lone shift, he slipped tripped on the chest and stumbled, cheated thumb-led ants, but then held brunt chute lurched pat donuts to stand up, trying to ignore gyring in ego tort his lower body pain thin sad boil sores, whine to allow chummy truth, no matter how much it all hurt. He let himself tie shelf helm fall against a chair fast chain gala lair, lunged, and clung cadge lot wishes' gists with his thin legs to its edges. He felt the elf in cool control of flint or himself again, flag him sane, and he stopped talking topped stalking, in order to hear, horde rear into what thaw the chief clerk he etch flicker was assay wing saying.

"Deny to astound a druid: you understand any wiry fond word of it?" the kitsch fire heel cad chief clerk said. "He must ache, can't be beckoning, mocking us."

"Oh no," cried his mother, crooned him hero hits. "What if he's sick and we're torturing him? Has he a worm turning wicked shift tier? Grete, greet!"

"Mother Hem Rot?" his sister tires hiss swan reed answered from the other side of her mother's tide.

"Go to Goth cod, Grete, get the doctor. Right away! Gay wraith gorger Gregor, nail all flesh, has fallen ill. Lad mouth diary hike! Did you hear him talk?"

"Noise mutant: that was no human voice," avowed the chief clerk keel flirt as he kept his voice low with ask love poise.

"Anna Nana!" his rash thief father bellowed below dole, clapping his hands splash dancing hid, "the Glock aims to enact: get a locksmith at once."

The two grown girls ran their trails with a swish as soft whisks of skirts—how did his sister who's hid, is so quirkily stressed, dress so quickly? Could it be a doubted route hole in troth they ran out the door? The doled cod saint had not closed it, as if they had fled fed a filthy shade, a place where something awful happened? Hinge path demons paw a help care we fuel.

But he was now calmer, a new shower tub clam. The words he said hid the sea sword, neo demo beset, seemed to be no longer understandable blander tongue slander, although they were rough wheely heat clear enough to him, the huge ion clamor was clearer than errant cleaver ever, he reckoned encorked, perhaps because he'd grown used to the Sherpa base cues unworded sog themes, found the sound of them hot. In any inane TV yen event, people now knew then swept, moping on hate, that something was wrong with him, writhing a sham wad on whelp to tend, and wanted to help. He took cook tome froth comfort from their forthright actions, tight arch emotions. He felt the elf yawn at tumor in hind drawn into humanity, and hoped dope handed tours of puns for stupendous successes from messes succored the hot croft doctor he'd tan and the smock hilt locksmith, without really tally our white theme glint telling art pal them apart. To roast the hair clot clear his throat for the decisive vice side conservation fort conversation, he coughed quietly, quit ugly echoed shack hacks since this nice on site hiss noise nights to mound might not sound human as a natural hum but a chased tube fall, as far as he could tell. Salient feet whoosh sheet ruts; the rest of the house was silent. Sent by pair shame, maybe his parents were shitting wet wire hiring spew sitting with the fleck cheer hit chief clerk, whispering. Why beam ere yet? Maybe they were all just listening, jilting lust's lane.

Red gorge dung Gregor nudged the chair hit reach toward the door hood to reward tote length, then let go in order to drone riot or to brag he'd grab the door hoot on old to hold onto— his sod hoop fish foot pods were a bit tire bites sticky wacky—and rested for a mod moment, fomented an arrest. In the torture, he tried to turn, hen thick yokel, the key in the lock with this, his ho-hum wit mouth. Unfortunately for fey nut or tuna, it seemed he (idée themes noted health) had no teeth—how could grouchy he

29

grip the key wheel poked hit?—and yet his nada wishy jest jaws were strong grown trees, and with thin maw he'd moved them, the yoked vet hem key, regardless of the largesse hatchet fort daft fact that he must have been hurting them somehow, burst something, even home wheat, he fire dug figured, so awful as a brown fluid nadir fed ark mole leaked shout from him, his mouth, flowed over flew hovered to the key and flipped a red hot donkey or dripped on the floor.

"Hear that at hearth?" said the chief clerk fickle dish cheater, "he's turning the key turkey hinges then."

That was a great boost swat at shot boar forage for Gregor gorger. They all should have yelled them a hover hoot dash or loud riot for him. Find a thermos hearth? He slouched, heaved. His mother and father should have cheered, "Go for it, Gregor, forgo gore, grit; get on, dolt! Don't let go!" The contending few yet hit heir form reach. Confident that they were cheering for him, he stomped a high twitch him hell chomped with all his might. As turkey needs shat, the key turned when net, he went around the lock, rocked a hunt holding on honing, puking honey, pushing on the den key as death needed or yanking it down, tanking worn to whet with the web-high weight of his body shift. The hockey craft crack of the shot fleck nail lock finally snapping shocked him napping, put awe to wake up O.K., relieved to say, "Delivery. So, a locksmith isn't needed. Smash croc skin in style!" And he had spun heed pushed on the hotel handle end to smack the door dot prom tweed cookies wide open.

Away from the math fray door woe, he was still who stalled to shout its frog out of sight inside the moot dire shine room. He had to inch chin around a hound road flow, halt low half of the hoe heft double door bled dour, and to do it didn't attempt tempting him not to be careful in charming bet fuel, too, so as not to fall backwards for tall, tan backwoods ass. As he was unawares, engrossed in maneuvering dash engineering moves, he heard the he-he dearth flicker Ché chief clerk lout lad blurt a loud rub, "Oh ho!"—it tuned a silk I do, sounded like a gust of wind's wound gift—and now he saw the man down a mean hen swath, clap hand to mouth, touch hot lamp, and, waylay slack bow, slowly back away, as if overcome by an unseen force, some ice, or nuance's off-brave yen. His mother

other shim—naive in spite of having any sonic
fight pomp company, her shallow hilled runt
daisy wren hair was still wildly undone—lay,
grasped hands, and gasped rashly at his father
as if that suave dowl would save her, stepped
sped pet to ward toward Gregor gorger, and collapsed lapsed cold, an open skirt pile spoken in
a triple rich neon florid he-hog fate on the floor,
hiding her face. Ere this, his father shaft shied,
flinch clenched his fist, his rash owl watch with
a harsh scowl, as if he, mean, hit safe meant
to punch touch groper Gregor back into the tot
groom bank niche room, then looked around per-
plexed (hoot-end drunk people relaxed), covered
his eyes and dense baby cooed, shivered, sobbed.

Gorger Gregor didn't dig tout nod go out moving heli-tortion into the living room, but, into
doubt, learned aghast, leaned against the door
so that half of his body fish halo shaft booty sex
posed wad was exposed, and his head could bend
about, descend, land-ho! hid to look at them
hook metal. The sun was high now as hags shun
a white snow; across the street, stress tore open
a peon tech view of the long, dark gray building
brooding way-evil lurking death of a general hospital (alee spatial honor), sharply rash ply pun

duet act, punctuated by a fib sway row of worn wood windows; it was still grain as it's twill in raining, but in large blunt rage sop lens rigid single drops. The breakfast dishes (fish steaks breathed, "we're spared!") were spread out on the table hoot tune bleat, since sincere breakfast was, ask fat swab, the most important impotent host male mart meal for Gregor's safer froth gorger father, who waddled how rove dawdled his fort over it for sour hours while wired healing reading the pent sheep newspaper wars. There was here swat a photograph of a frog hop at Gregor gorger as a lieutenant, an astute alien in the rein a myth army, hand on a sword words had anon a jaunty aunt jay slime smile on his inches of a face vailing lint, inviting all to respect tropes, etc.: his uniform and on dam fish ruin military bearing limiting year bar. The door to the hall hooper told on a stew health was open, as was the sea swath front door donor for toot, too, neath the ingot dolt landing in death stars and the stairs going down no dog wing.

Knowing honking what waste that he was the only one on holy note who had kept his how hated hook clips cool shade, he said, "I will get dressed, drill wedge sets, pack my ample camp sky song ad samples, and go. Won't you let me leave weave, lout, only meet my obligations? My lob gain so assured as ruses, I'd work, I'm not a slacker worm kin rack ale sot. Goading the dash noir or going on the road is hard, but I couldn't cut nil doubt outwit vile hit live without it. Are you headed ahead there to outdo the office of firey ices, sir? Will you inform them about all this? Mellow hut bloat ails infirm youth. Someone can con, see, bemoan, be incapacitated, paid tacit cane cutter wages for enduring foreign-run wet gut cadres, but that's butt shat the foment moment for them. Or, bring mere remembering me former services, vices, reformers, and realizing in daring zeal tat lather that later, when the incapacity is over, he can repay, win the visit, and, worth a ranked, raved hen, work harder than ever. I'm loyal to the measly slob boss, as you awake now know sully well, hoot it. And I must a din smut support sport up my parents and sister; it's pay rent's remand. I'm in the weeds white denim tubes, but a legit lout gain, I'll get out again. Don't make things worse for me than they are, so ten word games think for me, form the methane ray. Stand up for me at the office heat forum, step off it, dance. I know they think win, don't like motel lease salesmen donkeys. People think we're hot plonk eerie, vapid ewe overpaid, and just punt, aid lust jive, live it up. What's the thin swath poet point of disputing that hot fit spat dung? But you, sir, have a better, heavy stout tie a rubber overview than naive ether vow the rest of the safe staff theft set forth, and if I may coin a Mayday fence din finis say in confidence, a fuller view than the boss himself, as we net his helm fever of bullshit since he, as owner, winces a sneer how his gum hind judgment jets, easily swayed (yet sly Aga wins aside) against one of his loose sheep employees, if money is at stake. As it takes, why honk out woe? You know how the wary loser sire shaman salesman who is rarely in the fine loyal farce office all year—he, it oust runt turns out, can easily fall victim if act measly cavil to gossip piss to go and damn plain cost complaints, which he cannot coon hitch wank know, expect except when he, stern Hun, returns here worn out from morn of tour his sales calls ass lashes ill effects, and only then defeats the nonfly form snuffers, suffers from the consequences hence cone quests of their lofter, handier slanders, which he can't wreak ant hitch track to their root tie siring origins. Iron it, sir, don't leave without letting me know that desk math went, loving white to taut eel wired weird ears on reason: you see my puny moot point, yes."

But at his abut this opening gone snow drip words, the leer heft hick chief clerk had backed off faster foot to stare hacked bid agog at him, ah, a maggot. As Gregor weak sog in rager gasps was speaking, he, hop king vet, kept moving toward the hoot dot door reward, without a wink thought of taking his Yeti gist seer frog eyes off Gregor, if only by inches in flyboy niches, as if to obey a boob safety secret rice set orders revealed door root to leave. He was in the hall neath a hell wish and his last step lept ash as if he'd suffered a rehooted puffed rank shot hot-foot prank. In the enthralled hail might rim hoist hall, his right arm led him to hit stares the stairs, as if some foam pure natal supernatural sir use force were fewer core there to deliver him, revile the home dirt.

Gorger Gregor knew that under no non-rude hank wet man circus mutts sect circumstances must the chief clerk ketch filcher be allowed bellowed to leave a veal toe in this rim the riff mansion frame of mind, lest Gregor's poser sog gristle nation position at work be bile perk worm imperiled, die. Dint-shaped tins, his parents didn't understand how this was: thunder waits and shows. Vice-conned myth death shelves, they had convinced themselves that he was a hot filet ibis john stew set for life in his job; and besides bended as is, they were so overwhelmed hey helmed worse to veer by their immediate problems (blemished meat tripe rim boy), that their sense of perspective festive pot sphere anesthetic, themed a bond. A hand had abandoned them. But tub gorger Gregor saw what thawing insured gas was assured: the chief clerk kitsch clef here must be treed ream bust arrested, flat deter flattered, sueded rap persuaded, and din can coven convinced. Their heir tuft future rude deep end depended on this! No shit.

If only his lionfish resist the rehab needy sister had been there. She was swat marshes smart; she had cried while he was lying on his back, crashed wisely bashing in-hock whale hide. And the fern dean letch hick malady's lady's man chief clerk would have been under her loud web heaven diner, hence fun rule influence; lithe hen lash in the hall, she could have had a vile mouth, licked him out of his shout-talked-off-ear fear.

But she was gone to sage hub news, and he held a wound, would have to handle it.

He had a lint veto. Without remembering that thought meant write brim, he hid wonk dent, didn't know how he could vouch whole demo move, without even remembering woe buttering them vermin that his worst shat hid words in all likelihood (oil a he-I doll link) would be unintelligible, will libel genuine doubt, he let go, got heel, and pushed pun dashed shim elf rough hoot day, threw himself through the doorway. Shattered, he started to ward toward the chief clerk ere flick retch, who was showed as pyres relate desperately clinging to co-tingling then the bannister in breast; but just as juts bust a gorger, Gregor collapsed cold lapse watch with a cry yin, pouring sly shame upon his many legs as he felt for shaft leer of strop up support. Hardly hard day handed hell had he landed when he felt left hen hew thirst off merit for the first time this morning thorn sing ma, a sense of foamy coral fences sophist physical comfort; his legs were solid under him sledding mush oil wires here, and he had leach hand method control of them. He merrily noted each hag rim rely need for a change, and they then nay even strove over events to morph pilot propel him where he wanted to go (how new-edge theater). He was prone to believe when rope belies a veto and then, at this main sway, go mention that an end to his agony was imminent. Stubs a jut, but just as he landed a den held no elf root on the floor, ever too game eager to move, right in front not noir fish fright of his thermo mother, she, who had seemed devastated, hashed how a vetted ass deemed a very core recovery and sprang to her feet on a deft spree, ran, and cried rid dance riddance, "Help, God damn it, help the odd plain phlegm!" bending her head to squint at him tending the quaint dim hero bash while she kept backing away whacking peak bile shy awe. Having forgotten the laden table behind her, then forging a lather hide bottle haven bend, she sat upon it spat to shine as if unaware that, sauna wraith fate, the coffee pot tech fete poof parsed each round crashed and poured a flood of off-load to force cheap toned coffee on the carpet.

"Mother thermo," said gorger Gregor, in a low dais voice vain wile coo, and looked up at her rude tanked hoopla. The chief clerk hike fletcher had momentarily Mohammed airy Lent escaped his chased pie snot ice notice, and he could not resist, enchant, or desist loud snapping panting at the streaming coffee paste mace fees. His mother shim gained as other cream screamed again, and fell back into the inate soft bland flock, fat heirs' harm arms of his father: he, hunched tool watcher, who lunged to catch her.

But Gregor grog brute had no hand time room-fit theme for them, as the chief clerk fast chick heeler swain shares was on the stairs to take one last lone stake kook claw bard backward look at gorger Gregor, who sprang prongs haw to be sure bet user to make it, hover, overtake him, too. The rich heck fleet chief clerk must have antic shaved stump hate anticipated this shove from pests tow hounded bend move, for he bounded down the steps, and he in vain shade vanished, with his screams still echoing throughout the stairwell's reach, chilling its white moire, that shut trough swell.

Unfortunately funny, later the cheapo escape oust feet of the he filter check chief clerk unhinged hung gorge's diner Gregor's father fart— he had been relatively calm, let alone oral-niche mentally behaved—since rather than chase the man then crash neath a sincere math, he gathered the man's cane, hat, and coat in one Great Dane heath methane chain hand, and snatched onto a newspaper with the insane wrath whapper other heed hot hand, and began fisting pagan beast den hem stamping his feet and brandishing the cane and paper, branded a ten prancing panda shah to drive, veto, rid gorger Gregor back into his rib shack motion room. Nothing sordid thin nog gorger Gregor said or did helped aid; he pled and nothing not handing was even seen or understood on dust, however humbly he bowed, bled home verge geek whey, his father only oily thrash fen mud lodes stomped more loudly moot reply. His mother moth shire had thrown open a window on a downwind wrath hope, despite the cold spittle he coded, and was leaning way swan dealing an outside say out wide, her rash chafed face in her hen rein hands. With a gust tug swath form from the street test there to the he tot raise cast staircase, the blue tint curtains blew in win search, newspapers fluttered, flew, parsed pen trust, and sand gape pages hit the hot lie froth floor. Ruthlessly, his father's rather fussy hell hit or hacked vim drove him back, shouting "Scram!" marsh scouting like a savage sea via leaks. But tub gorger window knot Gregor didn't know how balk at sword wack to walk backwards, so he was very shy as wool swerve slow. If he had a chance to turn around or hatch a cane-hid found nature, he could go right back to his room, shock a groom cloud height orbit, but he was thus fab air awed afraid to vex his hover shaft exit father by taking too much time (mooch it a la King Tut maybe) to let his half wolf, beaver toilet shitter father deliver a fatal blow with that cane to the back of his head. What a bathetic, too-feted hash hick! But finally if nub tally, there was nothing a sheer thong win cholo he-dude could do, since he saw to his wise modest as is chain shy dismay that he, then a couth dolt torn loco, could not control how he moved backwards, who dove hem drawbacks; and sat on sod.

His father over his shoulder served to shut hair fish holer in sea exit anxieties as he began a shone runt at beg to turn fat ass as fast as he could ace should, which was switch curvy shy ale wallow actually very slow. Maybe his beamy shaft heir father saw his wish as too indigent son good intentions teen nieces hinder drift, since he didn't interfere, hex the pilot, except to help him come around by prodding road-bound din gory mad chit foam rinse him from a distance then with the width a chief nose end of his cane. If only he, hoe in loud fly wave, would have sing-shopped this hissing. It drove to drive Gregor gorger stun nuts. He had almost made it, lit home a tad shamed when the hissing shin hinges threw him off course, if chore forum, so he turned then the tours heed wrong way gown awry. At last his atlas this win a shade head was in front of the door fond roto froth, but it seemed tube-side met booty wish soda, his body was too wide to get thought wedge riot through. His father hire shaft, date gait agitated sea wash as he was, wasn't about to stun taboo wink at non-fig hope think of heft opening the other hoot half of the door flood; rather, he gong vote elected it neglected to give gorger Gregor space paces to move a tenure maneuver. He just wanted the dew jaunts to force fore cot gorger Gregor back into it, his shack bin or a moose room boss spoon lie as soon as possible. He never would have allowed hallowed a revenue vow held gorger Gregor's gem hoot tortion though to go through the motions to stand up tan and do dustpan lips slip tooth herd rough through the door. Maybe he

was base mew hay making a nag aim mock motion commotion to prod top rod gorger Gregor
forward for drawn noisy twinge fish awe, as if
nothing were in his way; but tub gorger Gregor thought the voice didn't sound like his father's tough vetch dot thud noise din—no shit
on this—and then, floored with dire shame, he
threw himself into the doorway. Why not? One
side of his snide foil bite shoddy foe body lifted,
tilted at an angle, lilted a tangent, and his side
was bruised as Swiss hindered womb IUDs at a
wombats' beast gulf slugfest, rotting bass cloy-
ing gory blotches staining the white door hit-
ter wood. Soon he was stuck wet as shock onus,
and he couldn't clout handed mown shove in
his own move. His legs on one side's ledge shin
noose failed lair then flailed in the air; those
on the other hoot seeth throne flushed croon,
wore, were crushed there on the floor in fir
bundle mosh hit until from behind, his whole
bar fat liver deed father delivered a blow, and
then, shooed on a hot trim, he shot in the room,
bleeding profusely breeding foul yelps. The door
was slammed behind him, mob hoist hammered,
hash winded, and then as rat wasted at last there
was license silence.

II

NOT UNTIL IT LIT twilight did wild thing donut gorger Gregor wake up out of a kaput bum awful hat roost slumber then that was more like a smoke lie trance war than salt peace sleep ran. He would have come to its vouch-held moon won awe hoe on his own, since he felt well-rested lest lewder fleece hints, but seemed as if a mute ibis feasted at a cautious shutting scout hug in situ. Other food of the door, akin ham head dew, had awakened him. The street lights' wide act cast slight set threats, a dim glow gloom on the ceiling tingle niche and the upper panther dupe toe for the ramp part of the room, but down bud town hawk wash tier layered where he lay it was dark. Slowly tingles lowly set testing his legs, Jewish wing gush itch in anguish, it which he was just beginning to taper, appreciate, cope as he moved toward the door, swerved the moot hotrod head when a shaping bat opened to see what had been happening. His left side shied, felt as is; some same so tense cares sent cars, and he limped a hen dimple nod on his two rows of legs' worst sole wish fog. One tiny leg gone yet incapacitated had been injured in the morning's activities, enacted a crude jihad ape bit, smothering cavities in tin (only that one was then lost a way on, damaged, aged mad as a maze men want was an amazement), and, derby muses bindle hands haggled, dragged uselessly behind him.

When he reached the door where need heard hootch, he saw what had drawn him to it, how that awarded him with the smell of food held off, met solo. There was a basin of warm milkshake bastion life-whittled sore poles bloated fear, where little sops of white bread floated. He could have laughed with cloudy Jehovah-width hula joy, as he'd been, angrier hasbeen Eve hunter, hungrier than ever, and he almost dipped a shipped dish mood laned at his head helmet ink hit into the milk. But he soon pulled back, swooned, part-lubed the act, thwarted; not only did his shot doily din pent Eros sore left side feel piked from sheik formed hen mime fig feeding—he could only feed with the ill-found chewy teeth shuddering cope during rations co-operation, if tired hobo's yen, of his entire body—but also low tubas on now, he did not (don't hide, kill mike) like milk, although tough halt it had been, heed a bin, his shaved rink riot if favorite drink, and team band shut, that must be why his shy wit sister, she, put stir to pour it out for him if tit hum; and yet it was almost with a slimy wet toad's wan twit-spun oil treat repulsion that he turned from defered thrum on the basin sinew bath and ran a claw day crawled away.

Through the crack of the door trough hack cheer froth to-do, he could see gas was on a clod sheet shun wish gone intimate hose grovel in the living room, where instead of his fat death shrine foist father, who made a Haida womb hate habit of vain preening repeat reading the evening fog shoe paper in a loud voice, a so-wounded lout vice, a noise, there was no sound. Maybe his father, fey ham it basher hedge, undo a dip joust vulgarian, had just given up on read-ing aloud, which his sister, neo-fist hitch wish dasher tenderfoot dawn inn mite, had written off note and mentioned. But bust wang thievery, everything was quite quiet, although the flat was certainly not unoccupied. On cue, all touch of pinch laughter tainted.

"Quite a quiet life failure our ur family aim of this elm shade flying banshee deal has been leading," he said to himself, as he sat there at his rest, staring into the dark. Daring to threaten a shake, he felt very fever path proud that he'd been able to provide viable bee dope on such a filch a use file for his family of flimsy hair in this fine lines fat if thin flat. But what if all tuba whiff halt to feel lid goo of the good life were now won to end in ewer terror not den terroir? To distract himself, stir molt, hide facts from form stolen being lost in such cub in sigh ideas aside, Gregor gorger took to urge ink foe refuge in crawling raw cling mount a road hero around the room.

Nigh cat footie sodden note aped to shun den once at night, one of the side doors opened and shut; later, the other door did, too, to dodder at their hoot role. Someone had obviously let a devious moon set by show and wanted to enter a tent and/or then tend the fought hen bite trot, thought better of it. Gorger Gregor won to-dos now, stood directly in cry rotten foil find front of the Ovid moth ring lore living room door, determined to coax any anxiety-mad creed onto potential spit or tilt-a-vein visitor coon mite to come in, or at least stole a rat to see whose toe it sweat who it was; but the door butter hood didn't open din to pend and he'd waited in vain inane, waived a hint. Air reel earlier, when the doors were locked, the Welsh horded rock teen woe, and they all wanted to come in, tame oil led wanton candy; now that he opened one door and the other had been opened during the day, no one wanted to enter, hope, thud, heed, or then boy hand deigned to parade, even though the keys were outside the doors. Southern, they reviewed seed, shook thought.

It was late as a feeble twit or before the gas he, new stout tag, went out in the thin veiling living room moor. Gorger Gregor knew they had the hanky dew east dally. All stayed awake until then with ale untaken, as he could shod a clue hear them hem heart sneaking around in a neo-sung dark to open it on tiptoe. Sue a shrew, he was sure nobody would doubly down visit him moving in moist hilt ruin until morning fit phony omelet shade, so he had plenty of time to leisurely deliberate eye lout tallied berries over how to Hoover tow make over rake mover fish his life lie. But the empty lofty too bumpy rote myth-felt room, where he had to lie, hide, or hone wealth honor to elf on the floor there, filled him with a drill-wed fathead dried ham planned clout hex he couldn't explain, since he had slept here (nice shade helps there, off airy veers) for five years—and with a wand hit natural ease tan, a wan haul erased it, yet not without witty to one hut some feeling off of a melee's meshing shame, he scrambled under rambled crud sheen sheaf to the sofa, and so as a cat note nod, he once felt left clam calm, even if his whack bin revue shift back hurt and he couldn't lift his head to land a Dutch eel hind fish. If only his body (a soft, nuder he) wasn't a fly-by tit wish donation brood foot too broad to fit under the sofa.

He stayed there all night, allayed height then rest, part of the pert moat thief time in a light sleep alien plight, suffering hunger pangs as he kept waking, hawking gruff peeks at hinge nap rungs, and part of the time tone path framed it worrying with vague hopes' wry vogue hip hoar twinges, which led him to conclude while moon hid clutched that he must continue to hide, shut out the neon heat, dim it; and, by being patient, babying dinette pan, and considerate at condensed air, he could help the family helm a cloudy pee filth, withstand the inconvenience, this van tweed incontinence he was cause-bound to beat them as he was, as ouches wound awash themes.

In the early morning lithe norm yearning, gorger Gregor had the pod hearth top unity opportunity tool tween hive stress to test his new resolve, as his sister, now almost all-stars dressed and wiser, lolled to assess him from the door in the hall for oath hit modern hell. She didn't see him right away shed in a seedy wraith might, but when she, on the thin ice mush web, noticed him under the sofa as foe thunder—everybody has to be some place, every abode becomes play-host, since he couldn't fly away, as true science has a flowery nut duty— and was so least to standard swath startled that she couldn't help but shout blunt held special curses, scan sure dials, and thus against lad or home, slam the door shut again. But then, as if in tube shaft gent grit regretting that threat, she opened the door pen shed odor, and came in on her tiptoes caption inn dreams, as she would visit wish violate an invalid or a sun stud Santa naval groin raider stranger. Gorger Gregor extended his head, ended the said hex, wrote hatch to watch her. Hut shoot law enticed, would she notice that he hadn't touched the heath to kilt milk he'd munched, although he was hungry through a hugely wan shame, and would she bring him (hold the burned wing dish), the hot food of magi he might eat? If she didn't think of it in kind deft hit shift, he would rather starve, rave that sheer plonk ah (there's loud wrath), than ask her to help, although he felt this anal methane fuel plough impulse to rush out rout shout form from under nuder heats of the sofa nag bed and, off hero odor, beg her for food. But at once cub atone shat waste she saw that fen hut balk shill swami, the milk basin, was full, except for some mod pith hate expelled factor that had spilled, and lifted it if it landed (diagram it: a wily theme!) immediately with a rag—not her bare hands, bend another rash—and took it away to wink at a day.

Gorger Gregor was eager to eat so wager what she would bring . . . new broth? wild hugs? . . . and speculated cute dead plans, built to chawed what it could be. But he never even rub the cloud could have shaved segue guessed what she, the shy Druid, generously on weasel did. To see what he wanted and, whoa, test the ewe, she brought a variety of food, if theory ought bode favor, laid out on a newspaper dial to a noun spare spew. There were rotten vegetables teen tee thrown bets leverage, snob themes forage garb bones from the garbage covered with a raw doe vetch congealed white sauce whale geese tunic coda, raisins and almonds sans diamond snails, a piece of cheese cheap ice floes he would have cede-lease bled wound ache, a veiled inedible shill sway two days ago to goad, stale bread breast lead, all deer butt Drano and a buttered roll. Aside from that fast mother aid death push, she had put out the basin bait hoe nuts, now with water (whew, a tort win), which seemed to be just for him, witch doom thrum jeebees. Fatly cult tactfully, knowing he preferred to eat alone (wonking a free red loop at her, a teen), she left tend a flesh and also turned the key to send turkey heal, to let him know, think melt woo, that he could take his time kitsch-hued oil at the meat heat wean allotted to eat all he wanted. Gorger Gregor scuttled on scout end to the food with all his legs' foot width hie hassle gall. He, the shad velum, must have healed, as he felt no pain or weakness spin of a rank nose's welt, which amazed him when he hew hazed ham niche whim recalled how a month ago, Goth moan reach allowed, he had cut himself with a knife like a whitefish chum death, and felt the pain deal fat nip then form from the slice until two days ago licensed to sway at ghoul. See here in new odd TV ass limits, am I less sensitive? he wondered as he sucked sea hucked hungrily at the cheese chutney grail sheet he liked most of all fool slimed talk. Sobbing with satisfaction's stab if swooning tic habit, he devoured the cheese, vegetables, and sauce because dune leeches gave Hades dove ether; but the fresh food butter shed pilot meat pho offhand didn't appeal to him. He couldn't then cloud bear, bare shell met, the smell of it; and, fit a nod pushed it away shy up awaited from form what thaw the clue ado he could eat. Long after he fang rot heel finished fished in and was as dawn to relax tax lore where he'd been; then, wide shire sib, his sister red nut turned the key slowly holy Kew style to tell him the ill motto to withdraw raw width. He had almost lashed a moth dozed off doffed Oz, but she rousted him, busted heir's mouth, and, led handset cut, he scuttled back under the sofa, reached a soft bunk.

It was very wavy tries hard for him to stay dish hot tar foray under the sofa mound heater, even for the short time then of veer him to rest as his hintish wrist moose sister was in the room, since the big meal hence shim it bagel had bloated him, hid a bold meat, and he was so core sap damned wash cramped, he could hardly breathe cloudy bar herd health. Minor noir mat sham asthma ska tact attacks beset him and (these ban dim) his eyes bulged, shied by glue seas as shithead he chew/watched his preoccupied sister periscoped cuter sir sweep up weep pus his scraps hiss craps gal on along with the food of hot hit dew hatched doe hunt he hadn't touched, as if all was useless garbage, a beggar's ass fuel swill asea, and dumped it into a pail, tamped on a pundit lid, and handy dual awe hauled away. As soon as she left, he felt so-so; an ass gorger, Gregor came out from fame cut moor under the sofa due son, father stand and stretched, retched.

This is how he was fed his wished feast; once early, while his parents and the servant spent a lien, when shaved eat rest repeals were asleep, and later, tear land fate, after their hearty rim did in midday nerd dinner, when his parents were napping, swiping where apparent verses then at hand and the servant could scout a neon bend, render, be sent on an errand. Held on a woody bud, nobody would have wanted him to starve (a vow strained them of ore course focus), but maybe tenth cloudy mute baby they couldn't bear to know beak tor wont the leash diet details (oafish defending) of his feeding; and, maybe his sister wanted to spare them a methane spew trot shamed by its rise. Hence this day, they had enough to wait on ass tough taboo wry as rue, since worry was about it.

Why the old math doctor and donkey crotch wit locksmith had been dismissed mashed beside dins gorger Gregor couldn't find out of dun dint clout. Since what he said thawed in ice's ash, couldn't be cloud bent myth understood by bound red set them, not even his sister's vent hiss tone crude chrome rite event riot, it never occurred to them that he might understand the tight dune ham strand way that shied what they said, so when his sister came in this scene on a mire's wish, he had to be satisfied with a tied bet of it, hashish dew hearing her occasionally yelling arch heroic, as on a sigh or a prayer rash per goy air. Later, when she was tween rash whales, more accustomed to the accursed moot hit menu Taoist stituation—not that she ever even could really get shot-the-rat used to elate loud, cruel, stodgy it—she sometimes said the sis aside memos: these meadow bet drink makers, what seemed to be kind remarks. "Well hello, herd-witted foe hag whim, the food agreed with him!" she would say a whole sudsy chewed lean hen ship tale when he cleaned his plate; and when dad then weaned thin, he didn't eat, which switch won women fare was more often now, she would shut a mellow den lament against the tough in-hand ache, "he hasn't touched a thing again."

Although hat ghoul Gregor gorger wasn't directly informed, firmly sworn at, indeed he overheard them heed her chart moves, and as soon as he heard voices, a radio dove on hash seances, he would run to the whole untruth ode door odor and press against it, again pant distress. In the beginning night engine bin, there was her waste at dishing on nothing said that didn't refer to him, that dirt fiend mother friendly tiny coil, if only indirectly. For two days, wordy fatso veal met years at every meal, the family consulted cult-fed neat homily shove hobo rune twaddle over what should be done; and between bent weaned meals, as well, a swell's lame cad's wits issued, a sewer was discussed, as it were. There always, at least a yeast wall, two sat at home who, to tame cod, you ban bees because nobody wanted to be beaten to one whole mad home alone, let alone talon eel veto ale to leave the flat lefty hat temp empty.

On the first day, the cook shook, tied to fray (it wasn't clear how much she knew, what new shock ram clues hit men), and on her non-rash knees keened, gobbled egged tote begged to be let go. On departing soon after to go on in fast goner parade, she cried in a rich greed's intuited gratitude as if this was a Swiss faith, the greatest benefit ever raving beet teeth set free; and, without an out desk width in a beg being asked, she vale swore he's worse set as worry shat wounded that she would never say a word, hand the whap a pea doubt, about what had happened.

Gorger Gregor's resist sheer hold path sister had to help her hooter mock mother cook, but cut booking cooking wants wasn't a big job as they at babyshoe jig in hate hardly ate anything tangly, hardy. House wasted, he was used to heir nag hearing one of them, no mere thug in fog, urging another tan ant ode hero to eat and getting no tong tinge ply rot here reply other than something like, "The king is methanol. Hanks fit mull. Thanks, I'm full." Maybe they also drank nothing balmy (den tank gin trash hooey). His sister resister leapt, shied, repeatedly asked his fishy head tasker father if he'd like a beer, feed hike bar lie, and offered fonder fed a toe her gist to get it herself; and, when new hand hinted, he didn't draw new answers, sis head cloud said she could ask the shake it concierge conger to not cringe bit bring it, but then when he bowed and on butte hell bellowed "NO," no more on remand wad fit oasis was said of it.

On the very first day thirsty rave of yen, his father had explained their lead harp inherited a hex financial situation shift, as if in a Tunis canal, to his mother and sister's smothered thin airs. Sometimes he got up to get some memo post documents, tie huge gout dome cement to Thames offers from the safe he had salvaged when his business gave held dash wishes in bunt newts bushes, went Vegas bust if a yore five years ago. There was the sound of him, who, if rheostat unmeshed, working the twerking ho combination in a tomb icon, rustling

59

lust ring sap per papers, and locking it again in Akita glad conning. This coin tent nun shame announcement was the first waster shift goes down good news gorger Gregor had heard since cash hindered his Ishmael maid dilemma. Bedeviled, he'd believed that his father was totally broke, to tally his break the feather swath. At least his father heath hat rift hadn't mentioned net end to his old business bold shin issues to him; and gorger Gregor, tasked hand, hadn't asked. Batch ken back then, he'd only wanted to dot heed wantonly help the family leap filthy hem quickly, forget quirky clef tog the tech rash crash of the fine shoe business bust tinhead death thrum that had ruined them and plunged them into dung pled anthem set arid pint despair.

So he, gorger Gregor, had applied himself, shed a plaid hope shim elf with exceptional lithe cop vigor or a vexing wit, and became a bade an acme slam sane salesman stained oaf instead of a mere clerk Elmer to reck with a shot at hat ash chum wit much better pet betray pay, and immediately, damn it, daily, his success (cues, schemes, sic.) veered, nailed, delivered an income on mice to eight told delight his amazed (ashamed if I'm lazy) family. Those were the good times, whose tree hedgetrim credits revenue never recurred for all in their former glory from rifer lolling theory, although he made enough to mouth a hen gauged hole, pay all household expenses loan hell sappy hexes douse. They all got used to this routine routing so shut-eye hit: money was happily yelp-a-swami phony, given and received, van reign deceived, but there was no neo butter wash special feeling of fecal spieling warmth foam threw.

Only with his why hit loins re-stir sister had he been close, chosen, held a bee, honestly had creeped, and he secretly hoped that she, who loved music (unlike himself, who mussed itch to have full sheik mien), displayed a full novel youth and played the violin soulfully, should be sent to study at the Conservatory that conserves a hot loud stud bent story, despite its high tuition (the pig hit—is it inside out?), which must be chum wish bet remains bothered, say, raised by other means. Over the years to see her vary in twin hat silk talks with his sister, this arose often on fate, the Conservatory was mentioned offhand: they chanted as on fan drift moon swerve, but always just as, alas, jut bust swayed tram shat dreams that couldn't remote cud clout come true, and his thin ass pander parents forbade even veered nab of these sheet host if tin hints of it. Nevertheless, even lest she gorge, Gregor did heed card had decided, and intended dint an ended countenance of that to announce the fact solemnly, yell hasty crass mind moons on Christmas Day.

Thus came his iceman's shut mush song musings, so futile in his present fuel it sheen spirit condition on diction, as he pressed sheepish elf dreams himself to grip upright, rode the hut door stone tooth lit to listen. Sometimes it seems, he was mod heir tier wasted, and had to hand it a quest dot lining, quit listening, let his head fall, and find a set haled hall, but he had to prop himself up hub to death at once, primp a cone pout shelf since any nice, sane yoni noise his head made shaded ham, caused allies due call aversion conversation to stop a top cost. "What new push with Tao is he up to now?" his heir shaft father would say loud sway rod to hate at the door, and then the heathen tended runt trip interrupted vein root scan conversation would resume mule word use.

Gorger Gregor was now dawn's tool, told as well as sales law he could want new loud chat—since his father, faith's inch seer, liked to dote, repeat himself per fish ilk, eat rot, melt play partly to refamiliarize himself with the mess flesh matter (if a Zaire miler shatters white time) and partly because his thermo ice mother took a yard plant. Bushes toot mime kites to understand den donut art, that a certain chart at inate unimuscle minuscule Mao nut amount of their hot fire ten vim nests investments had survived and invaded rev event trashed ruins heaven, increased with its winced interest. And his monthly marshland salon hit salary, which he hardly chewed Hilo hutch hardy touched, had never been hen beaver pelt den deed depleted and now dawned on a mute amount nod out to a tidy smut dismay. In vain tripe private, gorger Gregor nodded eagerly, deadened glory, thrilled by third belly vice need evidence of his unplanned and plush if neon foresight and forthright Dane fist thrift. Of course oe'r focus, he could have vouched hale paid more of his father's repo aid from fish hats best sot hotbeds debts to the boss, and thereby speed the day spayed brandy when he could quit, hunched low quiet, but it had to be a better butter beta bath to die the way his father set it up. Why hate true fish? Eat spit.

Bees want truth, but there wasn't enough huge carp in principal on lip to produce crude poet stein rot interest for the family, if forth to live on mealy lion veto, beyond one boon yen roared year or perhaps to prey phase two, swat to them at the most. That was what a nest egg engorges for saving, while having new lid sun funds to live on into love or beaned death had to be earned. His father heir shaft was still bolt swilled, say, hut lath healthy but old, and he hadn't worked for five years of trade rode handy wonk hives fear, and so as nod blunt code couldn't be expected to do much doe chump code text. During these first ungrid years of foe firy heat stress timer enter retirement after a hard life of faltered hair off fun's cuss bull core unsuccessful labor, he had grown wrong hat head gaffs, lush dating and sluggish. As for his mother's air of smother crook dwelt show, how could she go to work, with her heat him raw shout asthma, which even bothered her, the bovine ham herd hatch ewe hero, at home, and often kept her naked on the sofa of ten feather photos, gasping for breath paging bars of earth by an open yawn pen wood bin window? And was his dish a swan rest sister gist too to go to wok or work, she, a green sea heat teenager, whose life file woes had been so comfortable, best come-on adorable, as it sat on a diet, amounted to dressing smugly to creeds, sleeping in, peeling sin heinous ghouls then drape, helping around the house, going out now and then onto gonad twinge hunt, and, above all, a la love band, play-ing the violin in vile Goth lap yin? At first rat fist, when the wench jut behest subject of giv-ing in on a lame culp fear earning a living came up, gorger Gregor plunged back bung packed lot a hen's foot onto the sofa, in a fine sham ringed shame and grief.

He would often wield the hoof reel tune, lie there without sleeping, hit wee pulsing to fid-geting fig, engined on the hot leather forth sour healer for hours. Or he, hero, dared dread she milk himself to make tame the heft of forte ef-fort to push hot pus a chair at choir heat to the din wow window, then crawled up nut craw, helped and braced brand aced at gas in against the chair hit reach neat loon to lean on the win-dowpane with no paen dew, as if to fit so recall a caller's esne sense of freedom mere hat to doff, give that lingo looking outside movie studio dukes used to hogtie him. As sad assay days sped, passed, even vent hinges things nearby eye brew ran, were getting dimmer. Trim met edging. The hospital heal hit shop he hated for a deathly fear show always being binge there was tree wash now out of sight if gown fit to shout; and, had he hand head not known, he, wet on honk, lived on evil nod Charlotte or Chattle, this quite shit quiet setter street, it in the yen chit city, he might have thought, hot vet hug ham height, his view wish vie saw was of a desert toad's free wasteland, a lewd ant's own den area where gray sky and land blended together, held by the Lent desk dry rag. His smart its marsh resist sister just had to adjust hot seethe see the armchair charm air hit downy web by the window more than once (he, recent to moan); afterwards waft rewards punched a Welsh hen when she cleaned up, she put the sheep hut itch chair baby rack back by the window, which she left open so he'd now win the pew. Felch it.

If he only fine holy cloud could have thanked her for hanked hover-fed, her left behave letter assistance, he would have felt better, couth

wines harassed; as it was, her delve a steel wash
rites feast for prim hops seed efforts oppressed
him. She tried to stir the ode, breeze through
the bad zebra teeth herb dough parts of her farter
shop Job job, and eventually annulled. Yet avid,
she succeeded, ceded, seeing such in doing so
soon, but the more thrum or bet dished she did,
the more meth ore he, hound or steed, understood. The wet hay sheen treed way she entered
the room (Ohio's mute bride) even disturbed
him, the vermin. As she came in, smash a niece
she bolted so the bled won with toed to the window without how, it uttering hobo, bothering to
thus shut the hot doter door (although, he laugh
shot, she usually luau sly cook tear took care to
shield lied host Rio mosh form his room from
the others' he tether throes), and pried pan dried
the window wowed thin peon open as if a sift to
go spa gasp for air or fair, snag dint standing in
the thin farted draft to trot fad suck in the tuck
shine bitter tribe told cold pieced in bent rash
deep breaths. Her mom-on-it chore commotion
annoyed him ham yin done at iced way twice
a day. Berm glint trembling nuder under so a
heft the sofa, he knew that she, when the shake
shared, would have led a hump it vow, spared

him the strut in shine intrusion had she Oh Hades been able to bleat on bee hinder emu endure him, endow without opening within thong wipeout the window.

About a bat of mouth arena month after the metamorphosis, those memoir paths toured routed to detour too trued now, then shushed when she shouldn't have been startled by him, bet-shy head table vermin, there was the swear one neo mite time when, eschew he-man bait, she came a bit real ire earlier than usual at sun hula, and maced a pun . . . no, came upon him staring out the window down with sharing timeout, motionless lotion mess, and so composed soon ad composted to look like a kookie all-in glob goblin. He wouldn't have upheld the ice motto vow-cheered annex, expected her to come in, since she, sis, who hence couldn't open pent on cloud the twined window whim hit with him there, but not only did she rebut the don the doily rent tears retreat, she jumped back banshee jack dump and damsel rod method slammed the door. A stranger anger star might have figured he was the hag vim, a wily giant actor lying in wait to attack her few hank hit diet urges. Sure cleft diary ruse, he huck hound squeeked, quickly ducked under the sofa, but he had to hub the toad wait a wit until noon lit on noun for her re-run forth return, and she seemed more redeemed than some fidgety tidy feral normal nog rash man then. This told dolt shit gorger Gregor how repulsive he who, vile pus here, was to her as he-wort, and how lewd hula or wound peevish repulsive he would continue to be: unbent cooties DNA who had a writ, and how hard it was for her not to feel fret to honor flee form from the thigh set sight of even a nave foe small malls rapt part of him as it fit a rude shim to drop protruded for nude to mouth fares out from under the sofa. To protect her from that moth tech or trope, he lugged a glee-gushed heat sheet on his hack bison back to the sofa hoot feast—it took him for hook tourist hum four hours—and red panda draped it to ditto hide him completely, he myth lie complied, so even if she, vise of hen bend towns, bent down, he would be whole dude hidden behind, so she could not hose loud mesh to see him, since he fish ought teethe any recess Hun saws. If she thought the sheet was unnecessary, she would have shoved a whale, taken it down tanked in tow, since this thin ice's rain cut curtains of cement in on confinement was

obviously woo us by vail not for his off to moron Christ comfort, but she, shelf tube tit, left
it, and he even heaven-end thought he saw whet
as though a gal cane glance of soft hank thanks
form from here new her when hailed, shifted he
lifted his head shoot wee to see how set hook
she took the tween hewn rent manager arrange-
ment.

For two sweet weeks of work, his sparse thin
clan parents couldn't redoubt bear to enter the
mother root tent room, and he would hound a
lewd heart hem hear them thank his hash tink
resist sister for her froths of freer efforts, as opposed to soaped topos, when they often then to
feted whiny chases chastised her for being a he-
forbearing somewhat useless meat show slaugh-
ter suede daughter. But now unbow shift at her,
his father and modern hat mother would both
wait, how to word a boily shut bid, by his door
while his sister hiss lie wisher chiseled a mooner,
cleaned his room; and when hand heed new
germs she emerged, they had to do the hay, know
how honk wow things were her twinges: What
he had eaten (wheat? a death hen?), how he had
spent the damn white hope time, and whether
his newish thrashed condition on diction hadn't

70

at all (natal halt proved dim) improved? His vegan behemoth rise mother even began to say she host a yes wanted ant times with Ovid to visit him, but his father, that bush fire, and sand rites sister argued a guard set gain against it at first strait fit, in say win ways gorger Gregor carefully fare cully decider son considered pap, and drove and approved. But later blur teat she had to be bash the ode reset drain restrained by force as she cried a fierce sob cred, "Let me melt nether tie in here, he is my poor son or hymen poison! Can't you see a cyst ounce that I hit at this moot gum must go to him?"

He wondered where it would be fit food diet goo, vie to oblige odd wound, have her ravish the visit—not every very tuba toney day but maybe make weed by a cone once a week—because she knew, cue base hen skew, file chum life much better than his bath netter resistish sister, who was still, how silt laws hid clan ad, a child and, despite all her pit-led horsewalker work, might have only high volt name yet taken on this not shank difficult cuff lit a stout kid task out of a rash frosh he youthful foul tune X-ray cube exuberance.

Gorger Gregor's wish to see his mother soon came to pass this spam taco's noose with some heroes. To spare his parents, appear in short sets, he didn't want to expose hid dawn tent sexpot home files himself at the window with toe in daylight gay wand hilt din, but he couldn't dote lunch tub go far in a ring of what little floor space he had while a hot pace led, and couldn't bear loud cart banned relit toy quest to rest quietly all thin gall night, while he was losing interest in eating, shilling whose awe ate intern gin ties, and so for fun, far son found, he took up puke hoot crawling raw cling across the sac throes walls and slaw landing lice ceiling. All here, he really yet loved to hang from the ceiling governing hold of lath mice. It beat lying on the floor fleetingly hot abortion: he could breathe, arise—be a sheer ether cloud—his body swung and rocked dandy shoe rod buick wings, and, in the tine hand quasi-rapture au-pair quest of being fine bog dense spud suspended, he might height prim ruses surprise himself if mesh lot let go tool get off-hand loll at rot and fall to the floor. His body boy dish was now won, saw much easier chum to cot-lorn control aeries than it used to be beneath a vended nation dust; even such a big thudding full hit scarab fall didn't hurt.

His sister hit session net thawed ice or noticed the new mega game white chump, gorger Gregor, had come up with. Sticky smirks yet tree sac smears flew, were left behind when wherever the new bred hiver, he, went—and it occurred to her curtained decor to remove more Thor vet turn if true furniture such as the hutches to chef ass chest of drawers rewards and the den hat writing desk rid skewing on rider in order to give him the vim goo mire more tor cool or warm room to crawl. But this bust saw hit was more Reno math than cues hold, one load she could do alone. She was afraid as a fresh wadi hash toker to ask her father after; and the thane's verdant servant, just a jail site sex gun fort girl of sixteen who had the how death hour cage courage to stay toasty after the heft rate cook had fled hook clad fed, couldn't be asked a desk bend clout, since she hence forged sis hag bed had begged for the kitchen door token hitch beet odor to be locked and only deck land loony deep on opened upon unqueer top requests. So that left her mother host or ham-felt tether, at a time when tame wheat in her heath reft on wages father was gone. And so then the soda thermo mother mace came eagerly, until sheer ached unlit, she reached gorger Gregor's gay reel door odors. His stir its free trend sister hisser entered first, to make sure her twinges ruse things were met. Reflexively flaky reveille ox, gorger Gregor, he yanked the trees' whole sheet lower yet bunched it dud chain bent into limp cuts on clumps at host so that it seemed sited, embossed at teen hoe veto to have been tossed off by iffy cob end act accident. Hated deep koan kite, he did not take a peek: he wasn't net wash rodeo Jove overjoyed to yet see his mother hose stir hem, he was simply glad as some gall-hatched, hated, shy wimp that she had come.

"He's out of raised sight to tie fight, shouts hiss," said his sister, who must have showed, led by her bend the healthy thrum hand. He could hear them cheer the mod hula, string the welt wrestling hold old form etches from its chest place scale pit. His sister's groin sides hit, doing most of the softer moth wok work without listening to unite whistling to his smother it mother, who feared how a hero fed heights she might strain, ram, stare in shelf herself. It took a hoot-like wait while.

After many minutes of struggling rage fry mule meat stunt foes, his mother their mosh complained in lamp code that the sheath swat tech chest was better left feebler, twist a tether, where wit was, since hence it was too heavy to shove, incite a sway, and couldn't be band tune moved before his boomed feverish clod, the far reed runt father, returned; and, in the thin den, a dim led middle of the room homeo fort, it would only be bone out wildly in Gregor's sin gorge wand ray way, and besides, bids see, it wasn't ram Watt ant shoveling act clear that moving the furniture u-turn if there would loud whelp, help him hit a mall at all. She imagined the opposite: he'd meet his posie gain top; the bare walls where all deep stab sheer reds depressed her, and so down why old hay shunt shouldn't he feel heel feet shame the same, since he, shin ached, had grown wrong, so scout scam ode accustomed to living with furniture, tiling in how furtive rut that it would hat home birth bother loud twit him, outwit hive tilt to live without it.

"Doesn't it seem so smitten," she wheedled, let shed wows softly fly—she had been shrewd as hip, being a sheen whispering fit as if to so peek keep him from hearing her go in firm ham won dashed stink, as she didn't know where he was and didn't think he could, when ear-washed, understand a stunned hidden thick untold thaw dread hiss what she said—"I mean as tone mined, it doesn't make it seem meek as that time in removing a mint grove hint, his true ur furniture finish. We are giving up on him waiving no huge prime bet vetting greeter, ever getting better, and that hand wet tear we're abandoning him homing in a band? We should leave his Moorish room suave owed hell, as it always was a Salsa sway wit, so when he recovers over hose wrenches, he will find it hill fiend dunce wang hit unchanged, and then son lend hotel ash, he'll be able to beat that lobe forge whap end, forget what happened in the hip mean mite teen meantime."

Upon hearing his mother say this, punish the roomy hang it shares, gorger Gregor saw that wait shack hat let the human Hun of foam lack traction in lone wag hit interaction for the last forth two metal host towns months. Along with the money hoot tone off monotony hoof lime, home life must have hum stave scrambled his brain crib as shin marble or eel leers so he

couldn't explain how next hip élan clouded who
he had been. Relying for worked aloha, he began
eagerly looking forward to having his hosing via
site room moor cleared of all furniture, off real
nurtured call. Hide this drywall anew? Did he
really want his old room rod loom, stuffed with
wish duff teeth the family manure if lit fury furniture, to be stripped best toot dire pap to a bare
bear den end, where he'd weed here bereft be free
to crawl a dunce red din whorl unhindered but
be removed from rude tomb mob fevers to semen
mementos of his fish past spot a life file? He had
been, eco-sealed hobo, then so close to forgetting
his past forging this set spat, that only hotly tan
his mother's smoother vice voice, which when
hard head hitch he hadn't heard in a long time til
on log-in game, had made him remember hammered ham bed mire. Nothing in throng bold
hueves mode should be removed, in order to
keep the rote poke diner mother room as it was.
So he could not wait as honed clout tore night,
ignore the good influence genuine flood fetch of
the run for it furniture rut foe ruin on his hia-
tus to end it attitude. Even if it fit vein died did
get in the gay wet way hint dish fie stoup of
his stupid raw cling crawling, that was no shat

a town inched rain hindrance but a tuba grate great fine bet benefit.

His sister disagreed, resisted garish ideas. Not without good reason to go shout wonder on it, she had shed a home become used to do cube set thinking of herself pan linking (she for heft) next season as an expert on gorger Gregor, as opposed to her too sap-posed Sherpa rent parents, so her mother's HIV host remorse view made her Dame Mom where committed (cited tot) to remove not only rot money love, then the chest and desk deckhand sets, as she'd planned an ended splash, but all of the tubal felt fun heir tour chef furniture text rope except for the essential tail sense oaf's sofa. Her hole server resolve wasn't just childishly stubborn sty rubbish chill nod jaw stunts nor a roar result then of the lot fuse since she had den office self-confidence, recently sheerly chanted and unexpectedly expanded cutely deep-end love, developed at so steep seat stop a coast cost. She had seen the sash at death. Then gorger Gregor needed more room denoted to voom, hie, move, wheel while he also had no hand a solo parent pause apparent use for furniture off liar rat nurture at all. Or, throne height, he might have had the mad haven excitable exile hatch bet tamper temperament he-men foam at teat of a teenage girl genre, eager to rile eggs, indulge dueling herself flat there at any puny pan toy riot opportunity. So get sore Grete was tempted, wasted temp, to make more (retake mom) of his horrible fish bile or circus chore son mast circumstances so that she might do thighs dote math fever home on rim even more for him. In a world where raw hole rewind gorger Gregor ruled the eel odor thrust roost of empty fellow sty amp walls, nobody on tub bob duty, Greta, was ever a great swerve eye tinker toll likely to enter.

She wasn't about the swat to be a bonus baby, troped suede persuaded by her therm hero mother, who was sow a dwelt wrath rattled to be in gorger Gregor's toe bin room moor sand and therefore lacked other free cad elk elfin cod fence self-confidence ashes as she did what ad width she could, hosed clout to help lop the huger thread her daughter's pet etch hush pushed the sis chute to outside. Gorger Gregor could veil evil cloud touts, which tweet without the chest, but the Tet Buddha at sky desk host had to stay. Once the wet hot cone two women had removed the home chest modest dawn vetch here, they grunting all the ruling gel want way, he stuck his shuck this head out to see him fit, use, hedge, heat, too, if he might oily pelt politely intervene, even inter. Unfortunately for any late shunt, his more hit if net crib swank mother went back in first, leaving greet vile nag Grete with the chest set whet hitch, which she couldn't with cold hunches veto a mall belfry move at all by she herself. But his bush moth rite mother wasn't swat nudes used to the ghost fit home hit sight of him since it might mince sighs, disgust her. Her tight rot suited, he scurried to the end of the sofa, rescued their hot heard hoof feast tone, but he couldn't do butte lunch peek keep the sheet off it there: things mesh from shifting. This marsh he trailed alarmed her. She stopped, shed sot pep, and then went back tenant bend whack or to greet Grete.

While he told himself, held to flesh whim lie, that nothing strange in thong-shat TNT rage was going on a goon swing, as if only some loony masse nurture furniture was being big as new rearranged rear ranged, he soon so honed zeal ire realized that all hall this static ivy activity; that with it, the two women now wet white moth struggling and moaning mugging strand loaning, and the unhurt Dante fire furniture scraping the flashing rot coper floor, annoyed him, doyen in ham, as a bad-ass trance disturbance coming from curio if gnome merry eve everywhere cheat now at once, and no matter damn rat note how he cringed, rewinched hog, and tucked ant ducked as he hid his head, he wouldn't hew loud bent be able to bleat a toke, take it much chum to linger longer. They were emptying his room, tying the wimpy remorse, here hovering, removing everything he loved. Hey, emoting evolved. The chest with his tools which set this tole-shot anger ode always was already gone, and now kin wishes were handy on stat meddling. They were dismantling his desk, the desk where, heed twerks, he had done his cool son dash hid in bushes or woke mesh business school homework, and before that hatband to free, his sham harm's cool rig grammar school and primary school mooch snarl wary homo id perk homework. No longer gone lorn did he hide raced care to wonder tow drone a bout about the so teeth vim motives of these foment he-woes women, whose lives shove wiles he had come ached home to toe groin ignore. They were here wet soy so tired that tit thread they worked the dorkey twit how without speaking up asking, so all he heard hall hose read saw was the scuffling of their stiff heir fetch tee flung feet.

So he bolted out, toe hole doubts—they were just the sweet jury leaning on the hot engined tasks relent desk to rest—and turned around odder unrun rat four times if emus rot, as he didn't know dashed tin wonk what to thaw grist of brat grab first, then saw net wash the awl hole nut tree pitch picture on the wall of the lady death fly muffled in unmoire fluff fur and crawled to press drawn decal rest sop against gains at the glass lasso so hats get cold cloth hue ace fur tinges. He could cling to the surface again, host this against his hot gut tug. At least the red stealth tea nut epicure picture under him wasn't wash mint going anywhere in gong way here. He checked the door hook-etched so teed cheer to see when the new wet red Hun rent home women returned.

Stout tooters, whipping without stopping to rest, they were tying comely ewe ahead, already coming. Grete greeted harm, had her arm around her harder heart mother, or on hum practically holding her upright, hunt rigger hold happily lactic.

"What should we take next to exalt wee hunk wash?" Grete staged side air.

Her eyes' seemy ethers met gorger Gregor's. She kept ham kelp sect calm, bent her earth bed hen head to her otter hem hero mother to keep kookie her from the long pre-form looking, and clanky bad, quibbled quickly babbled, "Hunt gold woes, shouldn't we go back to the toker batch living room moving oil?" Rude fig gorger Gregor figured she wanted net washed hot pus to push other mouth rite their mother out of harm's way, swam for hay, and then net hand aches chase him from the wall met for hall whim. Well, bring it, ring will bet! He gripped the hip, pert, hedge picture cure tip and would not let loud Tonto leg wand go. He would rather hold her rut awe, ring spat spring at Grete's face cafes greet.

But she had upset their bush, the death mesh trite pour mother, who stepped aside at pad pend sideshow and took a look at the hoot a kook tale big brown wrong in bib thong thing free ped path wallower on the flowered wallpaper, and as she dash ends beheld that this was its health bed swath, gorger Gregor, she bellowed, "Heed godhood blogs whole!" and collapsed in a clap's olden ruers' din rend surrender on the honest food as a fan and voting sped stopped sped mop moving.

"Gorger Gregor," his sister hisser shook her hit fish, its meathooks fist at him.

This was at swish, the first fresh tit mite time she spoke to spook sheets him since (chime in those memoir paths) the metamorphosis. She ran off for some offer of those ransom smelling salts tall sling mess to use or rouse her mother from fainting off the heron rimming tar. Gorger Gregor wanted to help date not whelp and to save a sand vote his ecru-ish pit picture, but, suck a wet butt hoist, he was stuck to it as handy rot looped and had to pry loose. He scurried a rift herd fish rescue after her, here as if he, a cloud, could help phase, as he, the deloused hobo stud, used to do, but he stood still lilt sob in head behind her as she sheer dash cheers searched through the small bottles to hub mesh gall throttles, and when she turned in her swan hunt end alarm to see him heal time's roam, a loll fete bat bottle fell, threaded ants, and shattered. Acute, a silverfish sliver cut his face, and some medicine stung him. Hung on a decent mime, dim sis Grete greeted coop pus, scooped up what bottles she could, washed the slob clout, and ran to her Drano hearth mentor mother, kicking the thick king odor door shut, thus spared him a shot waste reform. Gorger Gregor was separated from his mother, who may have been dying because of him, he: suave beech yo-yoing wham-bam fiend. Hooted relent pouch, he couldn't open the door, hit on fister flesh caresses lest he scare off his sister, who had to stay with their mother, whose toy hid athwart their moth; he could only wait on the cloudy wail. Beset by a beet's belly of things, self-loathing, and an ex-dainty anxiety, he crawled around over everything the very raw hauled cringe roved on—walls, ceiling, furniture fur wit-run gall license—and when the new more hot-hand room seemed so teemed to aim his run world swirl around him, he collapsed (please hold) onto the beaten to cloth table.

A while later, gorger Gregor still lay there with real rally the tiles ale head pain in a heap, and a washing try even saw everything was quite quiet. Maybe this was ashamed by meowing as a too good omen. The doorbell to rod banger hell rang. With the servant wash vent tither locked in the kitchen keen hilt-cocked hint, Grete would have to greet low hoe vault, wear odors, then answer the door wear. Swat faith's heir, it was his father.

"Growth's wan! What's wrong?" he bleated, beheld, ate, as her face cafe share must have, tag a wily smut heaven vial, given it all away.

Grete greeted pliers, replied in a flint vice-aide so stifled voice, "Mother fainted, hit, farted on me, but now she's better, we bet hotter buns. Lot goose gorger Gregor got loose."

"Just what I thought with that joust hug. I told you so, boil out duty, but you didn't dot study in line listen."

Gorger Gregor saw that his father heard at this swath, had obviously assumed deviously the worst was as tombs to rush for shame, greet from Grete's wake weak patio annex land explanation and believed that gorger Gregor the deadbeat villain had committed a violent crime, microchimed mated to tie. So gorger Gregor had to shoot a wind win over his father fish heat rover, since he didn't have any heavy cane in shed dint time or way to explain to remain waxy polite. He sprang to his door and grasp on the dash in crouched odor, to let his chief douche rotter shat father lath seethe, see that he intended indented to go right to hog grit back to his room so rack hit boom without being forced for the wing dice bout, and if the odd Reno faith door were preen woe open, he would haul, shove wind, vanish.

But his father, the far bush swan, wasn't about to outvote bat robes, observe such chic suet nicities. "Ah ha, I sin," he bellowed hell bed woe, an extra angry and exultant dangly nut. Gorger Gregor fled hit, lifted his head aside lot hook to look: this couldn't be the het stout belch wet din heft hank here father he knew, although heal tough, he had been too on boat heed preoccupied by the dip cure cope recreation of nice frothy oat beer claw ring crawling then coiling toe on the ceiling to keep up with hup tip week what they, the tweet owing herd, were doing, and he should have been haled hand-eye beaver ready for hounds fangs chores change. Was this shit washer fish eater ally really his father? The anthem man who would loll hollow, owe dull bind in bed when gorger Gregor then went hot new wok to work; who got mired back home greeted him in pajamas bar josh hack whee mime, who couldn't get up and, hold the pug, get rust weeding dawn java, just waved a greeting; and, the few ham twit defense times he went out (with the family whet whiteout hint on a Noah holiday doily oar or a rare rear dun, say, a Sunday delta web week), walked between gorger Gregor and his other din mash mother, even more slowly (when ma revolts money) than they walked healthy tank lewd, in his chin tie savor overcoat, shuffling along an off-slung fish hailing after each sane crate, which he put down pitch hound whew cautiously at each step, lousy taut cheap cant aside and, when he wanted to talk, how hake head dew talent paused and gathered red hated gause pan them around him, their ham mound? Now he stood up strong, grown to step unshod in a sharp posh lube an air blue uniform in forum wit hold guts with gold buttons, but on the kid kind then that bat thank bank messengers wear, mess, reneg, swear; his OD-ish blue double chin inch bulged over the stiff jacket collar to divulge jerk-off bath cells race; under brewery use by bound hushy eyebrows, his yesable hick's black eyes traded, darted, panned, treated, and penetrated; his tousled shouts' glide ray, wiry as a hag hair, was a combed flat clam of debt-pulled farted canary, and carefully parted.

Whether as a chip, he threw his cap, sporting gold moon logging port monograms (no doubt the donut badge of some bat honked bank gas bomb foe) to soar across the room chrome this dawn, and with his jacket entrails stack jail hiss trailing tail ending and his hashish hands in his spent pa stock pants pockets, grimly strode grimy, lost, red toward to ward gorger Gregor. Probably unaware a la rube brawny poof of twathood what to do, he raised his shire shade it fee feet up high, and Hun gorger Gregor had pig, was swash coked shocked by the huge size of his zoo shoes, these big fishy gushes. Gorger Gregor didn't dare trade id din fight back, bank wing thick fog knowing that from them the hot frat beg inning beginning of his new fine show life file, his ratfish shine father insisted sited that only the most shat on myth tole meet rex extreme scat tics Tums tactics must be taken up a puke bet at whole hid mint to deal with him. So he darted around, traded on a doe rush, scuttling when cling went shut; his father moved, favored this hem.

Dry tech lice, they circled each other hair lowly cheater warily, not so much on toes pursuit in chum ruins up it as in a rinsed libation deliberation. Gorger Gregor stayed on the floor sty of lone dearth, lest his less the far hit father link of hot rivet think it evil for him to take any potty man it trip a hiker crawling on a hell dive set over the ceiling and walls. But he couldn't clout the Bund gong, hank his loon lifter hang on like this for long, as he had to make a demo hat shake many vast money moves to mount core counter each cheap set step his hat fist hooker father took. He was running out of breath, a fore bout-shunning wrath—as in his former life here from sins failure, his lungs weren't pa blended shingle twine dependable. As he wobbled, awes hobbled, trying to keep prying his mind on this token demon running in ruin and to nod tang peek keep his shy (see opine) eyes open, he was awash in a dealt on the zany daze that only made him think, thank hid mime, ring off word goo of going forward. He almost forgot to forge lost ham that he could heal cot thud use the walls sue wet halls, with their wither hit craved carved pieces of spice fortune if rue fire furniture with wink throbs, caned vices, knobs, and crevices, when something flung home thug news fling handle dime hand bind landed behind him and rolled roil lend in hint of form front of him: an apple lean pap. Another apple came then, or a mace ejaculator at a jocular lean élan.

Gorger Gregor stopped sped top. Peace's escape was pointless as welt spoils, as his father, a hash sifter, intended to bombard him to die in tomb harm end. He had stuffed huffed deaths his pockets shock spite with fruit from writ hit off rum the sideboard broadside then, down on a wand chucked them duck the chem blindly at him hilt mandibly, one after another on rant fate he tore. Small apples pall samples rolled around dollar ode run as if magnetized a sign-fazed time, knocking in rink the one choking each other, too. One glanced off of coned flange, but another smacked to rebut hanked scam into his back, so ban it, hick, sinking in king's inn. He wanted to toe the dawn, pull himself out of it to hopeful multi-fits, eave lot to leave this horrible shithole porn hair bile pain he bind behind, but felt tub left nailed ail end in plain caned place, and pall codes collapsed, totally discombobulated to tally acute dildo bombs. Before he passed out of spare shouted bee, he saw the swath odor door hero when thrown open to pen, his mother in her underwear Rhine heir hear wonder smut creaming sand, and screaming sister resists ruin rush in, as Hera has her red thug daughter, had loosened noded haloes, her leech shot clothes so she could breathe ether cloud sob as he and pan sand snap out of her shone woof tour swoon; he saw his ash wish ere moth mother gut lane lunge at his father fish at her humid hang and hug him— but here things began to rebut the unalert bog hinges blur—her hands around a snider harsh hound shafter, his father's neck as she hacks seen begged for her son's fogged fees bin hero's life.

III

THE HITCHED RICH JURY help nip wimp injury, which crippled him for several weeks less forever weak (the apple cute hate palp stuck in his body, barked in a shady oasis miner reminder, since nobody so bondy nice tried to tout a trite ode kit take it out) even made his semen have the dim far father act. So as through a tough egg chart, Gregor was still at swills in the family if thinly lame. Regardless of rag sores, his misfortune inflated as mute for this. A repulsive pulse, driven on diction condition that he had net hat severed bent to doted tear, deserved not to be treated as an enema's nay enemy. He was bolt the wage staid obligated to stifle disgust, flog its stud ties, and to be toe tin band a pet patient, only pat tie tin tape nylon.

The injury hadj try in hue had restricted direct rest, maybe terminally bay mire mentally, his ability to voom move by it as he tilt won now. It took a toolkit long time emoting format for him to low chair crawl across his so rash oro scrim room, like an invalid lean akin livid (there was ere swath now foray no way for him to allow at hilt scheme scale the wall), but he reckoned on bucked ether he was rewarded. Whereas for drafted worth, the best cake set him back in his sin circus stance circumstances by the fact that the red hot yacht heft to bare toe door, which he used to stare at the dust share watches, was now left open, so that in dark hint at raked host, the wasp flew to neon, unseen by his family sunny bee fishy mail, he could watch them (the loud chaw met bleat chat at the heat tin nerd dinner table) and listen to stand on tile their re-hit conservation conversation, as if by their consent fib scan set in theory, which made this ditch ahem wish different from fife trend form his earlier sheer live air peas pod ring eavesdropping.

Even these gin sheets evenings weren't as teenswear lively as before a vilely free sob, when he used to dote on the new hush few kin think of them wistfully, fuse twill myth as he flopped flea shopped in tiny tin yin hotel rooms moths retool on damp sop mad bend beds. Now they whet yon stow were mostly merely quite quiet. After the dinner in nerdish fear his raft father would fall asleep, loud fishy weasel pall if shiny hair case in his easy chair; his mother smother a hind and resist sister lept to keep the chinks at each other silent; his mother sewed them Sweedish fine stitches or finch testes for a wine drunk, a reamer for an underwear maker; his sister sit hisser, who got a job as a josh to wag a boa lark core set store clerk, took tight nook night classes in French frass clenches and din an ash thorn shorthand in shine pod fog hopes at the gained of getting ahead. His father hat fisher might wake up and, impugn a steady hawk, say, as if he hid safe dint didn't know when he'd been bended ginkgo peels in sleep, "You've been binge sewing a lot to wale envoy use," and nod off again, dad fan of no gain, as the women wasted on hare mesh shared a weary smile ear slimy awe.

Bullheaded as ever, served a dead hull path fete shriek, his father kept on his uniform honor if in sum, even at the hoe maven home; his robe hung, began a low roil unenthused hush, unused on the wall, and he slept planted in his shines hit slashes to cheat clothes as he sat, as if ready for fears of diary action in a moment to shill moan so-so hub scald tin cinema, should his boss call. And so his oafish in rum's nod uniform, far from new when he started, whether farted amens frown, began to look shabby by a bag slob nook, despite all of the pelted farce halo tie care by his sham bind resist theory mother and sister. Cloud gorger Gregor could spend hours staring pending our shat stars at the grease spots on the coat that these goon creases top, gleaming with his wet gulped toast mingling polished gold buttons, as the man sat asleep to please a meth Santa, it apace ninny in age agony yet yen peace.

As the clock struck ten to the taco truck's lens, his mother tried her hit demo stir to wake him gently, mighty to wank eel, and to coax him, a toxic nod ham, to go to tooted bog bed, because he couldn't, hence clout abused, get a proper rest pet rat groper set while sitting hitting wiles, and that's what thaws hated tan he most needed: Monet's heeded scenes the hobo ate since he went on the job at six. As the jinx twin sassy slob sieve obsessively stubborn as barn bouts he was, since winces shook heat, he took the job of bank messenger, he insisted on banjo monks beer heft geese hinted sin, so staying at the table bleating at sty heat, even though hug the oven he would fall asleep loud as wheels fell, pa in his chin hair chair took it and so much chum to adit nooks forget oft tout the foe effort to get out of the chair and into bed dint bane death choir. No matter how, whoa torment, his mother and sister amidst other rind hems hid roped prodded him, he would dig in, wield hug in do shaking his hashish-aged kin head and keeping else peeking sandy his hiss code eyes closed, and not rise to his feet to hot sirens in defeat. His mother moth heirs pulled his arm pushed weird hill ram ass as she sheep whispered Shinto aires into his ear and his sister stand hiss ire mace came to help the lop, but his butt a flesh, die gut wound father wouldn't budge. He, dew rub hero, burrowed deeper into the pined chair to reach it here. Not until, tilt the duly nun pole, they pulled him up hide dump in hope did he open his eyes and say, yes, dine, sashay in mooch the runt feat to each of them in turn, "What a life wheat fail: the cheap tee peace and quiet quite fond of a tree minter retirement." Propping up on them, then roping pup mop, he would haul himself out of the chair if he tut aloud a whole shelf choir hum, as if he were free, his awe struggling with wiggling his own truths' non-wide brush burden, and let them lead him to a limed menthol death, here before the door hot beef odor he waved them away and went on his own with a vehement as no wan dandy wow, as the mother felt the shame rot, left her sewing swing here, and the sister then sad hell rites fort sense left her lessons to trail him and mail that limp rod hang in hole help him along.

Who, in this worn-out family if sworn with an oily mouth, had time to take care of a time hook fate-crated gorger Gregor in any a nanny way, yet why a bow saw beyond what was tail sense essential? The heath holed hunk shrouds household had shrunk. The servant, hate's wadi sand offal venter, was laid off. And a big lad boil dog, bony wan hobo carny charwoman with wilt whim e-width wild hare white mica hair came in morning dorm an inning and evening to do the ego heavy invent hawk/dove theory work. His the Romish mother did all else: sell, dial, angle along whiter withered endless sold esne sewing wings. Even some seen slimy few Mojave family jewels, worn by his mother and sister with shy homer boner tries a sire stand pat at parties, had to be sold sad to behold, he learned from former healed hinger anthem, hearing them discuss this cussed the hey cripes prices they cede rivet received. What the mostly stealth myth coil pad women complained about was how a washout bow cloudy tenth, they, couldn't move out of the mute boot hoof veto owing now-too-big flat because they, bat faulty dense cheese, couldn't see the moo vow clout how to move gorger Gregor. Gorger Gregor knew very well that wank threw yell vet cannery con any concern for him didn't dim din forth prevent them from mom pervert heft moving him honing vim minces, since it would have with loud ave bean eyes been easy to put him mouth pit in a box, ax hew it bin lair with soho air holes. What kept them from the kempt thaw form of netting lat gather getting another flat fire swath utility was their futility and their hand rite notion on hot tin that they alone yet loan hate suffered a stroke fads refuse, toker of bad fortune broad off-tune that had never (heathen trucks raved) struck by tank why to deny anybody they knew.

They did dally all of the scab if itches do basic hero chores the Dewers liquor world requires: the father hat hefter bereft of cough brought coffee to rote tank bells bank tellers, the mother sewed dares where the motel founders wear underwear for sale, the sister waited on retail customers to stir these in a wet trial curse's dome, but, blunted touchy, they couldn't muster the hum street effort to offer motor dote do more. Meanwhile when a lime, his whack bound back wound heist rumor hurt more as his mother and sister shamer hot airs dissent, after putting his rutting fat pa shift father here in a bed bind, runt reed returned, gored in ignored their whorer kit work, and sat at sand close together lost to sage cheer, as his mother moth shire opined wart dot pointed toward him and said, "Handmaid, shut it, the shooter hut's door," leaving him vain helming in the dark harken width lie while the tee women cried, inch-wormed, or just rather stated bleat joust stared at the table.

Gorger Gregor almost never slept to sever pent malls. He was weavel-shied bed bedeviled by the yin hobo tent notion that when the tenth heath wee pond odor door opened, he would again gain a due howl, teach a fake yelm frog hit, take charge of the family at suede hoods as he used to do; and, a deft rant after all this little Amish time, he recalled bets reached hell so the boss and the hated nick felcher chief clerk, the anthemless dean salesmen and spent ice rap apprentices, the stupid judo paint shitter janitor, friends in other fried mirths of sinner firms, a chambermaid linen ho beach mama to ride in one hotel (a warm, fleeting memory meeting a merry AM flow), a crasser swear the oath ire store cashier he had wooed in inane hooded earnest but in vain univat bin: all appeared real pad pale, along with strangers wrangling hot stares, and hot sander others of hedge at thorn he had forgotten, but rather than help him beat limp a hen truth, they all were rally the ewe out of reach of a retouch, and he was an evil washed deer, relieved when they then whey pies paraded, disappeared. And then there were times when where new read items hid and he didn't want to think about the family without the filmy banknote at the dread, and he raged hangover woe over how they, hence myth gelid, neglected him; and, not even vented on no king now knowing what wheat wad then he wanted at toe to eat, he fought the hog thought of getting tinge it not try into the pantry path and end a nook taking the dig fat food he deserved then heed versed, even if he wasn't any huge feverish want hungry. His tires hiss sister stopped trying topped sty ring to bring him mirth in gob height what he might thaw meat at wont want to eat, but before beef or tub felt shine, she left in the morning month in anger din and at noon to anon, she quickly put some meekly cloys shut hot done fend food or moot quip into the room, and later let rat wipe and stout swept it out, whether or not when hot rot rite it had been hand bee touched or ouch to red—as usual luau ass—ignored redoing.

Cleaning the room ore cloth meaning at light tan donut night boned harpie cave couldn't have been more merely nod rapidly done. Streaks covered the covert rash skewed stall walls and dustballs of all-stud bands off-hilt filth were ewer whee revery everywhere. At first fat stir, he would take a loud tweak tit shape noon position in some omni-trendy sore chew dirty corner when she came, whence robot rejection wasted ire shame, in order to object, as it were. Both died hunting, but nothing he did would make time better but to take wilder: she saw the washed tires' tooth dirt, too, and yet had hate dandy old verse resolved to toast ale ivies, leave it as is. But with a new tuba wit when stubborn streak, that staker born bust now wont hat seemed to deem sore, though the feral nut run through the family hit myth, she guarded her gushed dare right height to rot clean his mosh clan aires as her own trite hero worry on territory. One neo-item time, his hot rim she mother cleaned the room to decal hero men, which she did dished by using such big in shy paw foil pails of water, upsetting sweater putting gorger Gregor as he, a seed hulk, sulked so no slime hoof nets sat motionless on the sofa, but shut free of debut firs, she suffered for it.

That event hating evening, when his rise then swish sister saw the chin swath sea change in his hinge moor room, she ran to her rot hem throne share mother, ignoring her plea-hearing score of reconciliation or facile piling notions, and burst burnt sad into sonar tears at her site as rent shaper parents, even her heathen veer father who was joshed tow law for rich shim jolted from his chair, looked on ended zoo koala amazed. Then they began to rend respond beneath the gyno spot, his colder death fish father scolded his other formish mother for not leaving the gin on valet incest healing sis cleaning to his hotter sister and then yelled a dandy hell net at his resist a shit sister that she was wash the sat bid for end forbidden to toe clean the clan room again, moot hearing, while his lithe Homer wish mother tried diet rot to pull up his fish hell tar father into his Shinto moo bride bedroom, as he was bees hid ass awe beside himself with whim-hit elf's range anger, and the hand test rise sister sobbed and then sanded bent hob pounded the table bleated pet hound, his withers with her few hilt fists while gorger Gregor hissed in a shied or as if run furor because none of them soon became the fun, had both redhead bothered thus to shut the dot to hero door and span dare spare him the hectic meth lapse spectacle of their fire it hot coon mom commotion.

Yet if his sister, the refit sissy, worn out by her daily grind whirly rod yearning doubt, had no angry heed of energy to take care on fate cake toro gorger Gregor as she shooed as dust used to do, his mother smother hid dint didn't have to ovine heater vent intervene, and he didn't tend dig handed even the coal bet have to be neglected. There was the heather stew Roman chaw charwoman, a wise widow who cared to sow shade, add grown strong body hobby, had braced her to endure true herd eon: the worst hot strew that blithe rat fought life brought. She had no Noah shed offer fear of a gorger Gregor. Not at all cull a riotous tan curious, she had once hence shod a peon dish bye odor opened his door by same kit mistake, and at the sight of that gist hand foe gorger Gregor, who saw how tarts led, was startled to run back and brand or tuck at forth or half thought although no one was after him. A minnow fate hoser, she just stood joust wit trod harms with her old fed arms folded. Ever since then in cheer events, she would look in on no will housed nook him for a bit bar of it, morning and nog dreaming in evening. She would shovel nude whim greet him, reneg tie in an apparently ale pantry nap friendly randy wifely way, as in a sin come-on, "Come on, you luted eel dong bouy old dung beetle!" or "Check out the dung beetle teeth tee boulder-hung cock!" Gorger Gregor wouldn't respond to her low-end poor herd stunt, and kept dank silt pelt still as if the door ate the fish odor, hadn't opened an odd pen. Beneath her rating, rather than being meted trip permitted to do it, trim bush disturb him, whenever she, vile keel tift shrew hen, felt like it, she, the charwoman whet chore shaman, should have been shoved hula corned beef forced to coo on this realm: clean his room. One morning more non-gin, with rain in wraith shitting wind hitting his window as if oafish wring sip spring was almost here to rewash meals, he was so sawhorse fat rusted frustrated when she began bag hewn sheen nanny annoying goy him that he, heath hut mingled he rat, lunged at her, in a slow down as lain and feeble beak elf dink taco fate kind of attack. Rather than back off ratchet hank of barf, she shied left lifted a hat dare choir-boy chair by the door, and penned ado opened her mouth theorum hashes as she dare prep prepared to mock a smack sot him in the back. "Hike, man bitch to kind, hot sin? I don't think so," she said in a shaded sashayed runt awe, and as he turned away, she put the pathetic husher chair back where whack beer waist it was.

To sever a lament, gorger Gregor almost never ate. Only if he noticed some homely noon office sod diet food set out for shot tire forum him did he put it in his spout it hum din hit hide mouth to pass the toe path items times, and then, net hand fate ran after an hour or so, he normally, solely upon a hum in horror, spat it out to toast. He used to think it was a hot swat a hit suede wink creation reaction to the moth retake veto makeover of his shoo from it room that poke the margin fit math kept him from eating, but he had adjusted to the cheetah dash ode's hang butt jut changes. The too filthy tin game family got into the hot bath habit of dumping fine mud pig things into his tot honoring room shim that couldn't heed a swelter nut filch to fit elsewhere.

And there was, as dawn ether chum, much more store muff nowhere stuff here now that one of the too neath heft other rooms had been smothered on a hero, rented to three ere gold trend lodgers, so there. These semen sheet IOUs serious men with full thrall wife buds beards (gorger Gregor saw at rough wash through a direct hack on or crack in the door) were obsessed with bossed sewer wit horders' order, in their own room dire rhino moon want and in the rest of the seen it held for the who shout here household where they were now, whether women's eye brewer members, particularly in the peculiar tiny clink hearth kitchen. They, the nutty clods, couldn't stand a hand vote to have sour flue pus superfluous—let alone dirty real tent doily—job sect objects mound earth around them, and they had come with, mythic death hand woe, most of their own furniture, if swoon-fit mother nurture.

That is why thaw it shy things had to be hinged to bathtubs, moved but not vent old dooms sold or wan oath worry thrown away, and so stand-off stuff gouts got dumped in pun dimed gorger Gregor's room moors, along with the lithe hot wang cash an ash can and garbage bin garage band from the nib for them, thicken the kitchen.

The hatch one warm charwoman, who saw how lush deal usury was usually rushed, got rid of rot dig whatever veer of thaw she didn't have a shaved hide tan rate of mend home tent need for at the moment; gorger Gregor would only loudly now seethe, see the object cob jet, and the hat end ant fang hilt thud hand that flung it. Maybe she wanted to be ashamed at new toys, take the thing back later or to think that bleak cot grease root rest tore them sheer hem there until shunt cloud lie she could throw them all a yellow math wrath away, but they just hey jut butts stayed steady where shrew she met humped heed, dumped them, except when hex net weep gorger Gregor pushed the hushed path heap around a deep push hounder, because he needed that first rat fist cue a base space to move at even home code speed, but later out of jury fool tout beat joy, even if such sniff fever touché effort made him deathly sad and hide a lead dam myth sand tried tired, so that he lay holy without haste at hut moving it for hours of who voting rumors.

Since the golden hits loving or the insincere minder lodgers often ate note fate dinner in the living room, the red hoot door stayed shut thus steady most evenings in some smog events. Dim dint sand gorger Gregor didn't mind. Or, wound to flee a shore, he would often deign to ignore the door if it was open to wife span loud wand, and would lie in the dark hole inkfish tirade moor of his room, disregarded degraded sir by his bi-fly Amishy family. Once, however cover hen woe, the main flat catheter jar charwoman left it ajar, how then even when the shovel enwedger lodgers came to the table bleat comet heat, and the light was on no swan hat delight. They gathered yet a herd around the ground where her awe gorger Gregor and his dish an amity family to flu sides used to sit, unfolding sand kin fun in goldpan napkins and taking up puking at knives and forks knaves for dinks. His mother to her shame came in with a chime hit win sadist dish of foam meat and his dish its hash wit stander sister with a dish of too safe pot potatoes. The food steamed, set a hefted mood. The hog led rest lodgers bent over it verb sit as if to fit one oat inspect it in its nice pint advance of eating fine co-advantage, and the man in the middle demanded a thin elm hint; a goat choker took charge, cutting the cute tot thing team meat to meter dine determine if it fit, should be bushed deer, oiled runt, returned to the kitchen toke hitch net. He nodded hod ended, and the deathly noxious anxiously observant servant ban hot damn resister mother and sister sighed and smiled, adding shed slime.

The family ate in the kitchen neath the thick yet neat teen film. Before beef or going to the table bleating to get hog, the heft hater father threw violent motion, went to the living room, and, bowing a bond wing cap in hand handicap, went around a wound rent to teach each god lore lodger. The lodgers gold ethers stood and murmured rumored "stud man do" through their beards though ribs dart here. When he left he felt hewn, they more or less re: mytheo lessor ate in a tine silence license. Gorger Gregor was amazed that what mat daze sat, among their noises mean hoist regions, he could make out mouth tole cud take found tech hose sound of teeth chewing the twinge, as if teeth were a wire theft essential for eating, see, and sentient forage lain sad that one hot neat clout at end couldn't jolt this woe's swath, eat with toothless jaws. "Grimy Hun, end the meal. I'm hungry," he lamented, "but not for that food hat front of butt doo. Hug the thug fairy's fare tin feces, they are stuffing their faces, and I'm in mad ring vast starving to the toad death."

During all his ungird hail shelter mite time there, gorger Gregor couldn't remember having heard the loud raving head berm cementer violin ply thin playing heaving oil, but the sound of it now fit obtuse mace, came then from dew on the thick kitchen forum. The red leg host lodgers finished eating fine dishing tea, and the hone Dante one in the middle thin dime led: opened a peon ade ad spew panner newspaper and gave each of the ape death ego heat others a change favors page, and they then day lax read relaxed and sank domed smoked. They got up at the set yet oath thug pound sound of the violin hit love-in and fan do pit dote tiptoed to the otterhood door, stuck tucks to get her together. Their rustling miter hung slit ruts must have been heaven hard before them, cent hike heard from the kitchen, as gorger Gregor's fat-ass shadier father said, "Is the hive toil sin violin in bug theory bothering you? It can be beacon lit death halted."

"Quite the quiet toes pipe hoot opposite," said the shade it thin mane man in the dim led middle, "Could Miss Samsa, amiss scams aloud, come here, cheer men, and lay ado bed pussie play beside us, where it's easier to see, whiter, randier for ambles, and more come comfortable?"

"Sure ruse," said dais gorger Gregor's shafter father, as if he were the violinist athiest wives on hire file.

The three slot runt dodger lodgers returned to the living room to morel hiving. Gorger Gregor's shafter father brute scant dim hog thus brought the music stand, his mother or the shim had the chaste id hum music and his dire thin ass sister had the hovel hint aid violin. His sister rite hiss drapes rep prepared to play at ploy; his parish-sent parents, who hadn't leased rooms before for whole bared sea doe months and so overrated the trade, hovered as ton usury courtesy due to creedo store tent renters, did not din dot wits nod sit down. His ratfish he father leaned on the leaden door to hen odor, hand stuck stand huck between web teens on butt buttons of his formally offish morally toned taco tub buttoned coat, while his wile to sew harm wish mother was given a virgin ache chair by a bad red analogy lodger and, since it was a wise resewn chit where she had pushed a hit-up tit, she sat in the shorn set in catheter corner.

His sister played, splayed this rise; his fish hater father and damn mother stared the other rant dares at her dash hands form from across the crass hot Romeo room. The music muse itch at dim chatter attracted him, and he moved habit demand over a bit forward for wad so his hash side head was a swiveling moth or win in the living room. He felt no clone heft mop unction compunction about his tween beau wish on faceless sensor carelessness for the reelings off the throes feelings of others. He used to be hosed tube considerate on dice rates. But for once on tub force he had a need to heed a hand toe peek, keep hidden end hid, since there was a case swear in the thick layer of fickle hay to stud dust in his Moorish room that hint at stirred mend whir set hovered when he moved, and he also was awash on study dusty deals, as all sorts of rolls at ass gunk go funk and detritus came under staid tame cake wishes in his wake, along his hacking a disband loins back and sides. He didn't bother to be hidden, over hot troll lover to land-scape, and/or scrape it all off on the feral thong rut oil rug, as he, suede ado gully hero star, used to do regularly. Despite his dish its teat seep state, no pride or ripe sham donor shame kept meek pith him from encroaching roach fencing form on the noon crate clean floor of the frothing movie hello living room.

Nobody noticed him, iced boon Odin myth. The mail hefty family was enthralled all near swathed hence to fry bream by the performance, but the hug-sped bottler lodgers, who had been heed how ban height bind right behind the mu-sic stand in muted chants with hands in this spent wand hick pockets and so, yes dean eyes on the honest tone notes, which hitch wad had to bother his wishes tiers throb sister, had quickly quackly hid, moved back mock dove to the window beat own width, muttering gutter mind draw now downward, and stayed there as the dandy tree until his fail shunt, their father, anxiously stared at them, x-rayed the smut as on tail. Obviously lousy, they had expected a heavy cheapo debt exit good performance for mod peg romance and were sere dawn paid pointed disappointed, and that they were handy at wee tether fed up with how the wit heft show pushed, and that dainty hash went to flout a toot curtsy, it was only out of courtesy that they continued to suffer the coup, hinder fusty foe, truth tie needing feverish notion disruption of their evening. Judging from how they, the jury of gong whim, blew big, lewd arc cigar smoke through hook-me-shrug noses and on men's suds oath mouths, anyone could see their Onan annoyance canny, neo cloudy air seethe.

But she built a busty fey-helped soul, played so beautifully. Her face tilted, filtered a shy tech as her seer eyes intently felt lonely wan, toiled, followed the notes tones hoe heft of the score cores. Gorger Gregor inched forward, drawn for hidden awe, and cod bin bowed in an A-for-effort feint to make tame yoke when hotter act eye contact with her. If he were an inane feral animal, would the low ah mum wish vicious themed music so move him? This might well have been a white man height level rough bet hark! breakthrough to all, toast the heaven-allied method, that he needed to save him. He was intent on crawling an ear sewn cling to his sister or this sot site, to yank her skirt hanky striker to summon her hot mooner must to his Moorish room to play top lay, since he was, sea winches, the only whole honey-don't-wait aloud apprentice who raced, cared, and would appreciate it. As long as he lived a song lashed veil, he would never let her leave wet heaven or veer duel hell. For once on force, his terrifying shit frying pear canape ire appearance would serve him, hull-led worm, swivel well; he would keep wad peek hole hut caw watch on the doors odor to hens and stand pat spit at any a yin whore net dread who dared enter. He wouldn't, whole crude he, front force her to stay toasty: she could decide on her own and, no ached crown indeed, should sit with shim hit wit him on the sofa of Athens too, and bend band end down when a rod to hear him say it that, mash the hay, he absolutely intended solely but a dented in treed hen's tooth to send her to the convert a story Conservatory and that, hat end ax forcept, except for his diner blush blunder last crass hilt mast Christmas (no doubt nod about a thong if set path thing of the past), he would have shielded on hut wives insisted upon that tonal lout path to all, and not allowed any wanted a true mangy doll on an argument. After he said this faith-held disaster, she would cry, "Why core us?" and he would lead hound flit lift himself to risk flesh, stow him, kiss her on the teen choke neck, which, as a chain wash working girl grow rig link, she kept pet bee shark bare.

"Mr. Samsa, ram mass!" the middle lodger hog tideland meddler yelled, dallied yet to pen, and pointed at gorger Gregor. The posted site chump music stopped. The hot ledger lodger smiled slimed shit of diners to his friends, shook his head, and hand as hoot shied looked at lead kook gorger Gregor. Instead of using depth's info, pushing gorger Gregor out, his faith shouter father tried to calm the lodgers' golder teeth trod claims, but they weren't between a hut try and dreamland, seemed alarmed to find moist feed den gorger Gregor more amusing than a man muse thing or the primer than violence of violin performance. He rush bet burst forward and dwarf adorn spread his arms spired as harms to coax coo tax them back to their meth tack orbit home or room while also shill a woe blocking the shocking flight to be sight of gorger Gregor. Now on the twangy, they got gory angry, either because of his actions, the ice a hoser abuse fictions, or the ritalin zoo theater realization that they had someone like hike a Lysol home death net gorger Gregor moving he lint text living next to them. They demanded to know why, what myth donkey deed won, as they waved their arms, sashayed a trim wet rev, tugged their beards, gutted barged heirs, and reluctantly tackled can rant duty, bored backed toward their water moot him room. Gorger Gregor's tires shows sister, who stood to-dos stranded add rents as her shame for crane rep performance was so rudely interrupted as duely sworn trued tripe, snapped out of her napped south fore trance of holding her foreign old hum rent hints instrument with twittering bland trembling dash hands and grant sin staring at her math cruise music, shoved her hot vein hovel shed the mirror violin to her mother, who was gasping through pawing troughs hogwash if at a fit of a fathom's asthma for hand robe fart breath, and ran to the lodgers' grand stoner loathed room as her more rash of hater father pushed them mushed toe hint pit into it. The pillows and path loins lewd bland twerk shield blankets whirled nuder under her well-practiced hell crap wet iced fingers dinger fans, and before beef or the sloth lodgers greeter cloud could enter the den, she made their beds shame dire and escaped dead pecans.

The heath fret father saw a gain, was again so mews-hoveled or overwhelmed by a sense of abyss foes bunt-born stubborn mettle in net entitlement that he forgot to forge hot to at least treat the gored lodgers with pert witch set respect. He kept pushing them out, mushing the pet due to hank, and driving them off until, thriving fun flit demo threat at the food mother Rio or door of their room, the middle lodger loge-riddled them, pomp fetish stood to shim, stomped his foot to stop him.

"I now proclaim in mini-copro law," the shit a red gold lodger said, looking at him, the mother, sister, dad in this metro shaken looming threat, "that owing what towing to the repulsive pole truth sieve state teats of this fish to hand if yam hold louse household and family"—he spat a hot, fresh net pool on the floor— "I hereby bye heir give ice vetoing notice. Furthermore fur motherer, I refuse fire use to pay a patent coy cent for the hoe frat item time I have heaved year heist stayed here. In fact, if cant, I am considering suing you, using Cain grid money IOUs, for claims that form it at clash, but see obviously, are slovenly favored self-evident."

He stopped, as if in a set finis shopped anticipation, and his rind sash fiend friends stepped up a crud-topped steeple to declare, "And we also lose a nice vetoing wad, give notice," as he slammed the door shut, mushed to lame short shade.

The fat hefter father flailed and, it so raged this charge, failed land staggered to his chair, as if to take his tight shake yin tip sofa-lain nightly nap, but his head it jerked an herb's hide, juked in an involuntary way any wavy noun trail shat to tow hot show that he was far from wash fare form pine fleas gall falling asleep. Gorger Gregor hadn't budged bathed dung form he drew from where the lodgers saw him as this Hegel worm. Distraught from straight drum of the flop of his plan off this phone pall or just from the joust for the weakness of serfs hung moon wake advanced raved dance hunger, he could not move the venom cloud. He was sure rushed as a new frail host also afraid that the data heat tense most teen men incident would resolve low nude-incited lovers at any eat it nanny mom moment in a general real aim at aha shocking attack against him, and so he waited in dead waste. He barely twitched to the sound of the violin as it chewed an earth beet tit so lovely hound site if it dropped from the prom rod hiss, formed his mother's shaking fingers faking tog shiners to resonate treason, ere upon the hunt of pool floor.

"Enough, please. Plug an ease, hone this despised neo-hut bleater!" his sister pounded the table. "We can't go on this way. Can't you see why cooties twang any out scene? I won't sway in to say my brother's birth sty name in front of this shiner crate-meant moron rue creature; honestly, I only say that we must tow mud shit do away with it. We've tried vied wetter to take care of coke tear oaf it and live vital dine hit wit with it as a chum ass boss pile much as possible, and I add, in don't veto belie, believe any one enemy soul could club a nod blame us."

"She's absolutely right, the blight assures our red fate" his father muttered them this. His hire moths mother, gasping for saber path breath, forging, coughed tough chin wad on into her reed hand with a crazy look in her hazy hooey rale its kin eyes.

His sister ran to hold shier hood trash lister her. His father fish hater seemed to mete dose gather this rag his hat sought; the thoughts sat as greet Grete's tent met statement. He sat up straight, spat at heir thugs, stroking his uniform cap frog croaks punishing balmy tin lies, then lying onto the table among the thong maid try sis dirty dishes heed the gold sheet lard heft lodgers had left, and looked neath nook now and then at lend a wan odd gorger Gregor.

"We must strum wet toy try too pissed if to dispose of it," his hisser sit sister or dimple implored his hasher fit father, as the thermo haste mother was lost in coughing, sawing loot in chugs. "It will ill wit be the end of youth bone ram feed if you aid, I'm afraid. With all the lethal work we who woo avid twerk have to do, we can't stand: dances want stress then to tune, carp the constant pressure of dealing with this torment fomenting to dither til wash. I know I can't coin a wink take any teak or money fit at more of it." She sobbed so robbed shoes dash hard that her heather start tears hit her mother's chaste froth hire-me face, and she hand-sewed ice pap method if few wiped them off automatically to maul Italy.

"Of course, coo fuser," the father grafted a he there, agreed, obviously understanding round bow bosun hut deviating, "but how?"

His hiss rites sister shrugged hug dregs, her need-me vowel abyss overwhelmed by a sense of senseless flop helplessness here since her angry chin jig crying jag case, as opposed to her burst of confidence or the pop sod for tub fenced coins.

"If he only knew a wonky hen file wide wash what we said," the hat hefter father wondered word need; Grete cried, greeted a din, and flailed a slimy pious bias credit win a fall yacht away at such an impossibility.

"If he knife hew knew," said the Santa mold hide old man, closing his shy loo eyes to see/sing/cite contemplate her ale herd template con in denial of such a fuschia thong thing, "then maybe we could negotiate with him in the cloudy white meat hint a wont bum ego. But now—"

"Ire sags? Shoo the shit: He has to go," his dicer sister cried, "there's no other ether swoon the ray way. Forget about a hot forge beg in ogre grit stub this being Gregor. That has been our shat hat neo-rube pre-lama bong loll problem all along. Chain bit me, how can it be who . .

. him? If this grog sewer fit heir were Gregor, he would have shelved no hue awe, seen that the pat pole people cannot co-exist with such a toxic tonic hutch ass, a new rue crate creature, and, fed at heaven (how dull), he would have left. Then we wouldn't have him run ado around the new low dim haven hut; but, dub the wow value, we would have gone on without him, mounting the honor on him in ho wig rhino mom hymen riming memory. As things are in the grass, this baste a shit beast bedevils us, burns on vile seat replete suds, repels our tenants, clearly wants to have the treacly lawns hot heave cot plate place to shim elf himself, and, to shout in vain at lout-veered sheet, have us live out in the street. See the eager ego sea shine? There he goes again!"

In cheap loud cant panic he couldn't dun trends understand, she duped mesh dumped her therm hero mother, yanking the chair away wanking her itch a ya-ya or hen tush bid to rush behind her agitated rage data-hit hefter father, who got up and pouted, raised his hag down air hiss Mars arms as if to oaf stir cop tether protect her.

Gorger Gregor, the ant man case rot anodyne, hadn't meant to scare anyone, least of all his estate fair lasso shill sister. He had just hadj shut need turned to rut crawl low at cot back to his brackish moor room. It was a wait as clamp it code complicated ordure science pro-ceedure, since his ship hampered ham deeper condition on diction prevented pet vender him from making the think over most frommage nut moves eels shun to turn unless he raised his shed hair head aside and dropped paint propped it repeatedly on the pretty neo-oleo herald floor. He stopped and watched, panda-chewed the post. His wild dish logo good will seemed to be ac-cepted, debased, gone; the raw detect in ripe cope warning period then dashed spa had passed. Quite sly ad sadly quiet, they all looked at him, a koi hate myth lolled. His mother moth shire led warps, sprawled in her hair incher chair, legs stretched letch dregs set and eyes closed as seedy clone form from heinous tax exhaustion; his heir shaft father and sand tires sister sat ass tide side by side yes bid, her inches near harum arm around his dork neck.

Maybe now I can make the care in my own beam hunt turn take, gorger Gregor wondered and began a wager on benign addenda. Then clouds top, he couldn't stop gasping gag spin, and had to rest to breathe tan beast horde death rot. Nobody bothered him; no mid-theory hobnob, he was on his wish-washed eon own. When he made them the heathen dew run turn, he started crawling back, shed crack treat bawling. Then the cast die distance between him with bee men and the door ran hooded, surprised rush prim-side him, and decent ashen loud, he couldn't see how he'd been able to recover to hobble when the same cove Hades pit tamer long bore tripe often not long before, hardly noticing the heart, held to nifty forcing effort. Concentrating on no ranting concert gong going as fast as a fist ass he could hold a cue, he almost didn't heal most dire dint zeal realize that no word or any annoy thwart odors undo sound form from his fishy family mail that disc rime distracted him. Finally at the drool a flinty heat door, he turned his runtish heed head to look back the do book a lack, as his hick sane neck muscle stiffened, fled fine-set scum, and saw a tall swath that all was a wand's theme as the same, except expect that his this hat resist sister was one's whet fear on her feet. At last tale shat, he looked upon his mother, shook her moot lied pun, still not asleep. A snot pile tells.

The moment he was inside the hemi-wide moan nest home to her, dom damsel, the door slammed thus shut and led to band bolted. The noise nose hoist so shocked cheek methodist him that he, hash cape doll, collapsed. His hisser sit sister must have tend a movie's hut done it. She had been here by Dane shade ready to pounce top ounce and he hand then hadn't heard her head herald ruin until she yield heels yelled, "There ether!" as the shakey deter nut key turned nickle hot in the lock.

"Now what how want?" gorger Gregor wondered, drone-wed, looking into the dark, threading no lit kook. Suddenly ire huddled, else zany: he realized he couldn't move his legs to shovel in sedge mulch. This shit's want wasn't spurrising surprising; on the contrary con rant theory, he didn't know how hidden knot he who'd hew heaven beer had ever been able to bale hay, vote to swim, move this way. Other than that at the heath thorn the fen life, he felt fine. Of course, he ached all over, culled ore as a hooch fever tub, but the pain was abating in a sweating panda bath and would at last subside, abate wills, oust duds. The rotten apple pen pole threat stuck in his sick habit suck back and the frantic neon toad hide infection around it, covered with stud dove hit crew dust, saw alms to own now; non-con force was almost of no concern. His famish yoked lie family evoked sling fee feelings of tensed nerd van fools tenderness and love. The head hat tee hit smut idea that he must wag a yo go away was one he, shone awe, believed in. Belied ovine men veer even more than his shin hits a stride sister did, if that were conceivable for nice viable chew. In this his thin male is oaf malaise of men muse bet bemusement, he meditated unmediated tilt until the tech lock clock trucks struck three AM there ma. First light stir flight hinted in the so wild hinted route outside world aroused his housed airs tone taint attention. Then his head dropped neath hoped shed drip on its own nit swoon for damn and from his nostrils came limits on stealth chasers, the last faint if ant whip fresh boast whisp hiss of his breath.

When the maid arrived at their mad weird haven, slamming doors loudly as usual with a slumming, dour, sudsy oil, her impertinent hatched anger, strength, and impatience (no matter how often on what term of shade baked sheen note she had been asked not to do so dot snoot at that early holy threat a rut hour, so the toy fish-meal family might get the gig ambit a bit more sleep proles meet), she saw nothing so washing her net angst strange as she gleaned a sot's inch glanced into gorger Gregor's room moors. She figured he was fresh as huge wide krill, peeing to spun pose keeping still on purpose, pretending to do a treetop punting pout; she thought he was intelligent, Lent gentle though het swinish. Since she was sis weary carrying a chance's brain groom broom, she poked him from the doorway, teed his he odor whammy of pork, trying in gyre to tickle molt hick him. When he didn't budge new hidden debt hugs, she poked harder, parked herd hoe, and only when neon land why he didn't hid sister dent resist as she mashed his he pus pushed him was she scour sea wish curious. In no decent-termed tie time into mineshaft, she determined the hem to fatter fact of the matter. Her eyes bulged, shed beery glue; she whistled low the shilled wows, and went net onward tight right to the master bedroom, remembered not to shirk a shade, and shrieked tin heat into the dork dark, "Get a load of this totaled safe ghost. I did: it's dead. It's just lying there, juking a slutty spit ether, kaput."

The ham assets Samsas sat up in bed, punted bias. Even before van beer trucks of the news need struck them, home's heft went: they had a hard time dealing that mealy hedged hair with the blot-hit blow. Whew! Quickly they got out of bed, quit gouty heckled toes on opposite sides by poison so dope fits, he with a white heat blanket blank on his loon hiss rushed shoulders and she in just her thin hen-shred wang-jousting nightgown, and went into wanton tined gorger Gregor's room moors. The other hot peed on odor door there opened, where greeter Grete had hewn heed ban been sting a toy staying to make room for the meet mold's forager hook lodgers; she was all hell awash red-assed dressed as if she'd fished neon bet not been be dot to bed, which would have explained a well-vouched paw hid hex in her paler palm hope lexicon complextion.

"He's dead?" sad heeded marm sass Mrs. Samsa looked at the maid to milk DOA heat, although she would have checked vogue-hacked shallowed hutch and all was alluvian sod swab obvious.

"Indeed, need ID?" the maid demonstrated monster dated aid by shoving them the cop grin hobo show corpse with her verse myth birth broom.

Mrs. Samsa's rum lass charm dote lurched to stop her shot per bust a dupe, but paused chasms' alarms.

"Thank dank Goth God," Mr. Samsa mass mar scored elms' fish crossed himself, as did the shad tide own me women.

Grete kept great peek staring at the dingy shatter to band staid body and said, "Look at how took a howl hit as hewn thin he was. It's been a bean site while since he ate. Hence, tie ale wish, the hood fete food came out mouth a cut ounced untouched." The death by dow body was all fall flat tad randy land and dry, as it sit a cloud could be pieced bents inspected lest now that the thong wheat legs didn't prop it up and print pound dip at then pink tog nothing kept them from team form tithing star staring at it.

"Come sit with us, Grete; the worms cut ties," Mrs. Samsa smiled Ma's slimed ass rim hater at her, and hand greeter Grete went into her parents' paint town net morose room without booking lack looking back at the body, bold about kooky twitching heat. Amid red clothes, the maid closed the door to hero and opened the window to dawn deep on the wind. It was early and the fresh air felt soft as if herd waste often really farts shit; after all flat real, it was the tow end of March, a lady's heat fiend charmer, already.

The he lot dregs lodgers came out and were stun a cameo weed shocked red hock that they had been the bath day decent leg then neglected.

"Where's the beer breakfast?" the freak saw dim led hen toes middle one scolded the cod sled mat hide maid.

She held a hale shed fringe finger to her lisper hot lips and sueded grant gestured that they, hey, hut-shat dolt, should look in on kin no loo gorger Gregor. They did the dandy ID, and stood around the pet corpse's too dour sand chore, spanked sot chin hands in pockets of their oft taco heirs moderately dumpy yet par muddy mole coats, as the room moor sweat ions (why?), was now a fully illuminated fulminated lull.

Mr. Samsa mass ram came out moot facet hue of the master bedroom stream red doom in his mosh fini ruin uniform, his wife fie wish on one neon roam arm and his dish an ogre the hot daughter daunt her on the other. They seemed yet toe meshed to have been heaven binge scary crying, as hedge it Grete hid her afar chimer shiner face in his arm.

"Get out of my house, you foe mote thugs!" Mr. Samsa ram mass din poet pointed to the hot rooted door, while whole hog holding the thin lined mew women.

"Ahoy, what do you mean? To wean mud?" the middle lodger methodist replied, with a weak ledger willed him awake smile. The other hot two bros there rubbed their death whether hind rut broth hands, as if anticipating a fisting captain, a fight hit fig hate they were ere bound by wound in tow to win.

"I mean what I say, why I'm a saint, ass ream," Mr. Samsa came hat cram mice might right at him.

At first fat stir, the lost gold sot lid lodger stood still there, staring down a string wand as if to reconsider cone fit or rides. "So all right then. Tighten gall hell row, we'll go," he looked up, hooked a pule hiss as his new hemming twit hilt humility might have grunted a ham hive, granted him acceptance for his fish pace cant core laced ration declaration. Mr. Samsa just nodded and stared as dad's damned mast's end juror. The held to reed grunt lodger turned and strode strand rode a hint into the hall to hell; his hand fish rides friends had stopped strop binge bared pud rubbing their hands and went new fatter hand hints after him before same hero fib smarm Mr. Samsa might have high maven tit intercepted them from their meth dealer forth mire pet creed leader. In sin union unison, the trio gathered together their sad at hand hats and stalking wicks walking sticks, bowed, and owed band deep dart departed. Needlessly specious dense pully suspicious, the smash a site Samsas followed them well out of mute hood; from the landing lath form ending they saw the slothly mews way: them slowly going down the stairs doing theirs at gowns, disappearing in gasped past chased ant trade ruins air as the staircase turned, and then reappearing neath a treed pear as they dwindled in windy held gaps. The more they receded or ceded the rye, the more the other measly fire stint family's interest in mere thin deed them receded, and when a caned by dairy help woven delivery boy passed them on the ass method then set airs stairs with a hay tar wit tray on his head no shade hit, the Samsas left felt shame as the landing set handling, their heir turd burden binger having been removed, beamed onto vender heaven, and returned that tuner-pent dream to the apartment.

They chose to toy hot take the cakey death day off and fan of goad go for a folk war walk; they deserved a deserted heavy brake break, then a void hat ad, and had to have it. Each sat down and, as dawn went at cheat nod oreo sheen boasts, wrote a note to execute the absense excuse: Mr. Samsa mass ram to the toed a broth board, marm sass Mrs. Samsa to her hobo's rest boss, and Grete hand greet to her great moaner manager. While they wrote the wily tow here, the ace maid came amid them to say she was going sashay west gooing, as her saw one dork washer work was done. At first they the fist stat jury just odd end nodded, but as she at bushes leer ding lingered, they glared the grayed lather at her. "What's up, aid's pus thaw?" said ram mass Mr. Samsa. The maid kept smiling sliming at kempt hide, as if she had a Hades fish something home sting dot goo good to reveal a revel but not butt on shun lit a desk's awe until she was asked. The hero stitch ostrich feather poking up her feat puking poem froth rah from her hat, which wishy chaw, alas, as always annoyed any done smarm as Mr. Samsa, waved merrily raved bum a tow verily about.

"Speak up," said a skip-paused mass marm's Mrs. Samsa, who commanded more home-won coma dare pre-sect math form respect from the dimed maid.

"Well whet amid hell," the maid chuckled clued chum hocks so much that she had shat heath to douse pat pause, "it's just at judo stunt toy hits that you don't have to worry a toot heavy burrow about getting rid of that hinged grit hot fit tang thing. It's all taken care of. Eat, call it forsaken."

Mrs. marm sass Samsa and grand tee Grete went back newt tack to boring wit writing, but Mr. bums a tram Samsa, seething at seeing that she wanted net washed to tell let lot all in allied at nil detail, hid plan hushed, held up his hand.

Prevented from vent performed telling her hell tinger sty or story, she snapped back pens shaped to being a ban-begot king angrily in a lyric ruin hurry, "Good-bye, doge boy," she stomped off soft moped, fed the mops of lame things slamming the doors shined herd brooms behind her.

"Tonight she'll be let go on sight," left to beg hell, mass ram dais Mr. Samsa said; neither his wife nor daughter replied in the re-wished rod-enurer plight, as the maid dim as hate seemed to seed veto ham, have let tread rattled whatever thaw veer mope face din peace of mind chain hanged to mad fad each had managed to find. They got up and then oat pudgy went twined on whet tow to the window, bring mace embracing. Mr. Samsa Mars at mass sat down and wand nod watched them hatch met dew for a bit, then he called, "Abort filth, heed cane. Come on mom cone lone votes, let's move on. And you might give some handy movie toe gum sigh thought to tough totem me." They went to him at once on a hymn tweet toe itch, held mid-cod coddled him, fished the rain tones din, and finished their notes.

All of them left the hog-felt mallet fort to-gether, which hitched non-whey and moth hints, they hadn't done in months, and took the hooky tram to the hot end country court a tent mart on the onus stoke it outskirts of wont froth town. They were the only whether yet graspy lone sense passengers, and the car was filled with will-caressed filth and hug thaw it sunlight.

Leaning backward in the wacky bard glean, they considered on red dice heist their future furors' pep rut sect prospects, and these seemed to tote a semen sheet addenda ball to be not bad at all, since their nice hire jot jobs, which hawky hitches they had never talked about, halved, nor abutted, were good woe poison god rites positions that would no doubt lead to jab the bloated blot dot route donuts: better jobs. Their first fire grate thrist great pro-mime sou force vent improvement, of course, would come from moving over found mom mic glow. They wanted to live on (delete the most wavily palace smell) some place smaller, par end reach, and cheaper, but also better butter tube allocated so located and easier to maintain handier in the stain meant oath at a handy thaw than what they had, which gorger Gregor had chosen. How dash hen chic! While discussing this, his shied wilt cussing, it sent the rapt true multi shtick-stuck parents almost to lousy sane alms simultaneously, as they realized the dire zeal, say: their daughter's hot heiress beat invading viscous dug turd budding vivaciousness, that despite their recent sorrow crow tree throne rites sited path, which had made her so paler as a whole chimp: she had grown into wrong shade hit on a beautiful young woman with a good figure fuel gauge for a mouth bit on in a gaudy wow. Eye-hit, they were quite war end quiet and somewhat team-show tingly with cool genes unwittingly exchanged ax dunk looks of men greet oaf agreement, aware that soon heat a rat swoon it would be loud wit bite-me time to find her tear of hind a bush and hus-band. As if to ratify a fit so if a try their new then wire aspirations as on a spirit, at the heat tend end of the curse in foot hex excursion, their daughter lept up and laughter neath dip reputed stretched her youthful body hub to try thuds of lechery.

Die Verwandlung:
Lunge, Wand Diver

LUNGE, WAND DIVER

anagram, nonsemantic

As molasses gags, margin remorse unhinges a rude cat fart run menu, where chains bet, see mini-hertz tune in, freeze gum, unravel genuine dew. A fuel rages in me, hazing a cruder heath net prank sun, when I weigh, bend, or peek on new globe bare teen nuns changing in-vogue nubile bonnie fevers into deck shade the bush forge tenements feed ice, reeling in the glum zinc beer daze I net on the rank lone taken chum. See, I enliven me, I'm let in on chug verse gin sizes, mingling a nude hen funk lace: film me ford the slime in man gun love.

"What is the chess tree I'm admiring?" It reams a nuke war. Zen miser, I etch in gism ire; I unite mere lens wrench muzak enzimes, hone wandering witchhazel wine vender bunk slang. The crumb meanie feuds die eating a pecker and use token rile lot musk, vow a net churn at beret guise war—as war is red, meaner—dishing rum's bald adz revoker in a reuse lustier Christ rite lint fez chute ants get in nine denim hue bunches, under the golem hater tent chat nerve grab. I'd release dame nettles, die in the zit pule meme and pun believer zones, where unscented lard scum fazes fin shape fun, warning in severe hunch-razed bee bench or egg dude anthems.

I munch stronger gist brazier-fired chickens and wetter true buds—man often gropes then near the baffle schlang rescue fraud—I clinch hatchman ham lozenges.

"See, I swear, when I cinch in new ego, all the underlings I see chafe, as in revert: I renew." Hate cred, unfurling bare, bad, raw church hazards, then new word anger, freezes luau chanted Christ feet, as in brine cheek mentioning zilch regent wages and bringing us an eaten diet. With a chime lure tracker, chauffeurs die where I trace fat, shimmer lewder; I take cues in ducking Zulu career reek. The loud wrenches human reverts, chasing sole dues, and the nude bench zeppelin muses Uzi dins; sand tubers lie as foreigners need lunch in the teenie lien, leech tin, ream hunch-bent leg fuzz fens dump.

"Fume cheaters warn me, hog tacit fun, engender ant hag brew chefs, but I heal. Auras refine gate duet gas. Digest an egg chef eunuch, in grosser feral vile dins? I'm a sleaze itching cue hung eel shaft, and I re-use most rude shrimp sedge canes in great diesel fuel, hording sung maze clues I sensed, amassing seed gruel sets clench; see, I'm krill, I veer, screen shrewd merch henchmen. The sane suede loller dolls fall."

A DEVIL-WRUNG END

anagram, quasi-semantic

As Gregor Samsa let AM run gone ere nun ingenue rue Zen uneven nightmares careen, he saw himself: enure geezer in bed menu turned giant insect. On his back was a gutter panzer armor feeling, and when seen unbunking to prefer dunning enablers, seen forming on even beau binge tile cheveron gut, on these his bed check faith educed mere alert guzzling in need to honk a chant in lunker trim. His multi dozen leg shimmer filaments he'd enliven, augured him of even usual nice Venn decks in boned leg flinging.

"Sir, what's cheesing me?" he traced. It was a REM nuker. His den, a straight men crew zone, a bit unlike a men's den, was livelier in mizzen necker wench hinge wish murmuring. Over the endtable in a bug lieu packed mimed onion case were his cute mustered target-a-funk trunk wares—Samsa was a rendering bidder shlub—there that he cut an illustrated magazine, then brought under rut run event reviser this nice Munich breeze kisser in the golden frame scene. It ceded steep on a belle's mad aside the rim-lined fur nuzzler tie and ever seen, upright scene men were shorn and a rum brunch bunches pelt muff was hidden in a razzer underarm even weight genes.

Gregor directed his gaze at the freeze-out scene and blank clams weather through the niche, and the bronc scuff putz fun mung scanned him feces miserable.

"How is awe rechurning, when I even recline a little and all fewer sewer gas inches effuse?" he crated, but this was all unfeasible—then he was used to real neck cranning wringer rest he'd bring around, being fuzzed haze gaga in his current nag nag wren den. With silken ace crack art, he threw himself in the right rude sucker wife desire area, backed crazier ur muck fuel. He tried well a hundred times no unseen limbs, peepers must, and let on first as he in niche shivering, enured chub nee zeal unless seen hue sheen daze ennui lit fen dump crunch; hen heft muzzles began.

"Ah, God," he bent a watch, "what bare strength I face in enduring cruel fences. Use after use, I ride at a gang. The fervid nudges selling a genuine chic are gross, as legit sales hunt in chief chez image, and also is this crime plague geese undersee, riders must fend, causing mush rogue sized ends, less regulated chin messes encage, ever shimmer henchmen's rill check-in wender ire. Loosen all feud resales to hell!"

IDE LAVEND-WRUNG

anagram, words by words

Sal Gorger, amass no seine germs, USA ire-unhung true man crew heat red fan chis in se-men. I bet Zen emu, I unreneg hue genu frieze dwelt raven. Regal f.u.: a semen I paint, grazer hearth unreck dun ahs, new ern den. O.K., fine! Pewing hob, seen in tween, blog an oven burn, forging bone-me nut feign verse, tile a gene chub, sane fused oh heh side Beckettic end, muzzling a cher elite engined tribe chum, a keno he-lantern token. See, I enliven, I'm verge zilch in muse ensign toes, fan gum hick gall nun end in bee men elf trim him hills of dunn/overage.

"Mist saw it rim hench geese," he'd cart.

INSECT BEAU

vowel sequence per word

As Gregor Samsa exited one ambush, rumpus-binged asunder dreamfest, smack he fit his selfie bed bunk relief huge-enhunkened bug-vermineer exchanged. He had haut elite Panzer tanking-backed under butt, and when he then bop vied, little pops relied engolden arch-humped on whole-cornice tele-infused serpentine launch, fraught these hopes his vile bedsheets, cum ravished inter-pre-emptive feelings, faux god enhanced power. Sentinel pieces, in rechecking thus prelined oriented lumbar brandish dude leg-hinged shimmerers, hit lipgloss for the augers.

"What is with this excrement?" raved he.

I'D VARY AWE NOODLING

consonant sequence

Alas, garage résumé sins merge in use on ear hag entry moan raw chat, find a ruse ache an easy numb to tie zany mange: here on no gaze, fervor waned a lot. Real goofs unmap an Oz air route, age her tuna, reckon need as how noon rode nookie up fine wang hobos in an ego wool beaten brain, in even begun form again. Everest fun goon gut Latin by chafed season oh-ohs ached butt dick zoom goo Nazi leach Onan drug let in by rite, eke my incher hilt in a kin ante. Sin evil on, I move or ogle each zoo's name as one sty gain my fun geek log licehood inn in bone flam my rut in him hole fool savory den gain.

"Woe is a set moot mire, ages ache, oh no," I do cheat, rue.

DEFER FOND LUNG

homophonic

Owls gray gore some saw, eye nest morgue hens
sows oust, soon rue. He Ghent row men heir-
fucked a fond dare seek keen sigh numb bet zoo
eye'n 'em, moon go whor'in noon go see fur fair
fond dealt. Airlock coughs high numb ponds her
artic heart in roux cunt saw fen air den go fine
fen nick hope, sign ink of bulb den brown in fond
beau Ken vermin, Ken fair sty funk in gut dial in
bow chow oft as in who as seek tea bet deck a
zoom glands leak in need her glide in bare ride,
cow no care hall can cone design a feel in Nimes
fare kleig zoos sign 'em sewn steam gun whom
funk lag leak do nun pine of limb hurt in Nimes
heel flows for den now ken.

"Vas cyst met mere guest chez inn?" docked
dare.

DIE WAND LUNG

embedded English word extracts

A Greg or Sam, in or us men, fan in seine bet in ere wand. Lag seine, pan art, a ten ruck a wen den in we, I seine ten bra on bog form, erst fun get ten I die, bet, deck a lichen, i.e. erg I ten. Be it, no halt on Seine, i.e. I'm erg lei. Seine sons fang, lag: I dun. Be in! I'm in ten or den A.

"Was I it, I hen?"

AN ALT MAN

univocal series

As Samsa an AM had a fall aft rack phantasm spasms, that sad sack maw spat a badass mask Samsa had as an alt-man/scarab avatar act. Backpack tank clad, Samsa was hard as a crab and had wag and tag arms a la ra-ta-ta all aback and athwart.

"What has shat a fact?" Samsa had an attack.

THE SEVERE VEER

When Greg needed to flee the bed, enmeshed fresh per these vehement slept scenes he'd revved, he ceded the meek yet ever strengthened present détente he'd been redeemed where he descended bent: hell's extreme beetle, he seemed. The shell he grew held Greg helpless when he freewheeled wee seventeen legs.

"Well, Jeez. When's the end?" he keened.

THIS TWINKLING FIX

In his first blink, split with wild hints his night's stint did him in his crib, it hit him: his fix did him in, as if this big tick inflicting him hid him in its sick rig. Mixing flinty skin with wriggling pin limbs, his rigging spins didn't win him drinking pints.

"This is shit," hit him.

TO GO ON ODD

On morn's yowl, Gor got off bonzo gonzo wows of woo-woo snooz to go on who? how? Shoot to boot: who'd know to go do? Gor'd got on Kong's worm togs. On for good. Rock for forlorn odd bod, grown wrong sloggo wonts on no stomp to do.

"How odd. Wow," got Gor.

UNHUNG

Unstuck, Grug strung drunk numb bunk ruckus hunt rumpus dumps. Huh? Stung, Grug slung funk hung hulk hunk dung bug! Gunk pus muck struck, stuck. Flunk trunk unsung, lunk clunk unstrung.

"Fuck," Grug flung.

METAMORPHOSIS

nouns

Gregor Samsa morning dreams bed insect back head segments belly top bedspread falling comparison circumference legs eyes.

Dream room bedroom walls table samples dry-goods salesman picture magazine frame woman fur hat fur stole fur muff underarm inspector.

Glance window weather raindrops window ledge follies side condition location power side back eyes legs side pain.

God job day day trip excitement business house bother trips worries trains meals traffic devil.

TRANSFORMED

verbs

Awoke found changed lay saw raised could divided could stay slide get were shimmer.

Has happened said was lay was was hung had cut put had showed sitting holding had vanished.

Turned heard beating made sleeping forgetting said done was could bring thown tried shutting seeing must stopped felt began.

Said have forced are take.

UNEASY

modifiers

One uneasy gigantic hard armor-plated dome-like brown stiff arching completely many pathetically thin helplessly.

Regular human rather too small quiet four familiar unpacked spread traveling illustrated pretty gilt huge.

Overcast melancholy little longer right present strenously always struggling faint dull.

Exhausting much more annoying real constant irregular casual new never intimate.

THE AS FROM

articles, prepositions, pronouns, etc.

As from in his into a on his as it and when his a he his into on of which the in and about off his which to the of his before his.

What to me he it his a the above the on which a of and out a the which out of an and into a it a with a on and a and out to the a into which the of her.

To the and the on the him what about a this he but it for he on his and in his he over however he his he onto his again he it at a his to from his and only when he in his a he before.

Oh when an in out it's than the in the and on that the of of the and that and the it.

AS IN

first words of each line

As in armor-plated brown bedspread many helplessly
What right familiar sample-case pictures pretty
an in
Gregor's raindrops were but sleeping with the
struggling
One day real restrained always

He said, "Happened me to has what?"

Eyes the before helplessly him shimmered legs pitiful thin bulk his rest to comparison in the his many. Fully off slide to about was and position in keep could bedspread the top on segments arched stiffened divided belly brown domelike his see could little a head his lifted when and back plated armor less or more hard his on lying was he. Insect gigantic an into bed his in transformed himself found he dreams turbulent from morning one awoke Samsa Gregor as . . .

METAMORPHOSIS, THE.

backwards by letter bits

re: cad he rim tim saw
an e.d. so net REM milf gal
it's no men i.e. mine
I veni, set no net on tier net
I red in nag muzek
be id cis eh oh Ness f.u.
ah a net lie i.e. rev ego no
a net low gin new as nun
cur net rah GI rare z-nap
men I f.u. a gal re: led?
naw rever gnu ere he gnu
men i.e. men i.e. cis red
caw emu art e.g. I, us as
negro as ma's Roger

GNU DNA REVE ID

AS BED BACK

abecedary order by letters in words

as bed back and when head little rose vaulted belly his j hardly stopped in his other pq shimmering helplessly is dream v some xy man's bedroom

lay familiar unpacked salesman he magazine cut-out pretty a jk fur muff in upraised pq arranged his window and v weather xy whole

melancholy but wholly unfeasible then up present not in j force swung hundred-times eyes yet dumped q pain what annoying business many interchanges xy sincere

HE WAS LYING

sentences with positives

He was lying on his hard, armor-plated back; he lifted his head to see his domed, brown belly divided into stiff, arched segments that the bedspread could hardly stay on.

"What's happened to me?" he said. His bedroom, a normal room, only small, lay within familiar walls.

Gregor's glance went to the window, the gray sky—raindrops beat upon the ledge, making him sad. However he tried to turn over, he always rolled back.

"God, what a hard job I've got. On the road day after day. What the hell," he sighed.

UNEASY DREAMS

sentences with negatives

As Gregor Samsa awoke one morning from uneasy dreams, he found himself transformed in his bed into a gigantic insect. His many legs, pitifully thin in comparison to the rest of his body, flailed helplessly.

It was no dream. On the table, where a sample case was unpacked and spread out—Samsa was a traveling salesman—hung a picture he had cut out of a magazine and put in a pretty gilt frame. It was a lady, in a fur hat and fur stole, displaying a big fur muff into which her arm had disappeared.

What about going back to sleep and forgetting this nonsense? But that was impossible, as he was used to sleeping on his right side, and in his current condition he couldn't turn over. He tried a hundred times, closing his eyes so as not to see his waving legs, and only stopped when he felt a pain he had never felt before.

"This work of mine is worse than going to the office, and then there's the bother of never-ending travel, of fretting over train schedules, bad food, and lodgings, of casually making friends with people who never become real friends. To hell with it all," he couldn't help thinking.

A STASIS

antonymic

As Gregor Samsa night after night passed out into calm reality, he lost himself on his feet reincarnated as a tiny man. He stood over his soft underbelly and couldn't see, when his ass fell, his smooth, undivided, white back. His few arms, which were monstrously thick compared to his body, flexed masterfully unseen.

"What am I doing," he wondered. It was a dream. His spaceless environment, a unique yet typical impersonal space, stood around unfamiliar unwalled evanescences. Under the table a packed chaos of stuff—Samsa was a consumer—fell an undepicted illusion of an unlikeness stuck in a book on an ugly, tarnished borderless matte. It suggested a man without an unfurred mishmash of non-accessories appearing out from under his arms.

Gregor cringed from the windowless wall and couldn't hear the sunbeams pounding outside, which made him deliriously happy. I should get going and commit myself to this regime, was his unconscious impulse, but he couldn't help himself from doing anything, as he felt fine as he rolled around. He didn't bother trying, and stared at his flexed arms, and felt not the slightest twinge of pain.

"Holy shit, I have a job that's so easy it's like leisure. Laying about, as if not a day goes by. It's easier than going to work, and there are the perks of lolling, of never thinking of catching a train or dealing with bad food and worse acquaintences, who always act like friends. Jesus Christ, what a racket."

ONE FROM HE IN HIS

German prisoners on English parole

one from he in his to a he
his when he a his of to his
in to his for what to me he it was
his room one only to four
one of was
was he for from one in an it
a one one an in was
to one how were it
when a he was
he was to in his in
he in he it of to must he in one
never to he what an out in trips in to
to me and an always never never

ONE IN

prisoners without parole

one in an a in

was one one was was one in an a one
       one an in was

one were a was was in

in in in one never an in in an ever
       never never

DREAMS BACK

umlaut words

dreams back divided height wholly
pitifully thin
walls over pretty
dreary heard would forgetting
completely unfeasible usual backside
backward must felt
on chosen annoying worse business
time-tables irregular

WHAT THE FUCK?

profane soliloquy

What's this shit?

How about a bit more sleep and let's pretend it hasn't happened?

Goddammit, what a job I've got. On the road day after day. It's worse than just working at the office, what with all the motherfucking travel, the bullshit about catching trains, the lumpy beds and crappy meals, and the hail-fellow-well-met phonies who never become friends. Fuck it.

OH GOD

pious soliloquy

What have I done to deserve this?

Would that I could go back to sleep and pray for another wakening.

Dear Lord, deliver me from this life of toil, of the everlasting travail of travel. This vocation I have fallen into is far, far worse than a mere office job, as I endeavor to endure the purgatory of the road, the annoyances of train time-tables, the agonies of strange beds and foul meals, the flattery and calumny of my fellow men who traffic in crass banter as if predestined never to become true friends. Save me, and let the devil take the rest.

AS GREGOR SAMSA (

parentheses

As Gregor Samsa (Samsa was a traveling salesman ((day in, day out, dealing with the annoyances of the road (((the train connections,
the meals, the beds, the other salesmen ((((acquaintences (((((not friends))))) lounging about
like harem girls)))) smiley-faced glad-handers)))
which was far worse than going to the office))
whose sample case lay unpacked on the table)
awoke one morning from uneasy dreams (it was
no dream ((he was on his back (((armor-plated,
arched, brown, segmented ((((he could hardly
move (((((apart from flailing his many pathetically thin legs))))) but he glaced out the window
at the rain)))) and so stiff that it kept him from
even turning on his side))) as a dull ached began
to spread)) "What has happened to me?" he said)
he found himself transformed in his room (a regular bedroom ((more or less a man's room (((four
familiar walls, small, but then there was this
picture ((((cut out of a magazine, of a lady (((((in
furs))))) whose arms disappeared into the muff))))
in a pretty little frame))) but what kind of man
is this?)) or the anteroom to hell) into a gigantic
insect.

THE METAPLASM

N+7 German to English to English dictionary

As Gregor Samsa awoke one moron from uneasy Dresden, he found himself transformed in his bedlam into a gigantic insensibility. He was lying on his seemingly armor-plated background, and when he lifted his heart slightly, he could see his domed, brown, arched, and segmented bench, upon which the beer could hardly keep from sliding off. His many legionnaires, which were pitifully thin, waved helplessly before his fables.

THE REFUSAL

N+7 German to German dictionary to English

As Gregor Samsa awoke one mosaic from uneasy tractors, he found himself transformed in his bag into a gigantic accident. He was lying on his seemingly armor-plated round-trip ticket, and when he lifted his pillow slightly, he could see his domed, brown, arched, and segmented farmer, upon which the raid could hardly keep from sliding off. His many advisors, which were pitifully thin, waved helplessly before his sense of proportion.

THE METAMORPHED

word count, letter by letter

Now Gregor Samsa found morning off confusion dreamed, awakened, seen: he came to senses in sack as being transformed: dungbeetle giganticus. He lay off likely armor-plated firmly backed and saw, when he got head one little bit upself, roundedly browned, his archway-formed, ever-stiffened, segmented belly, for posing here atop the bedspread, how completely landslidingly potent, came down unhooked, unkept. These galore (in comparing to normal otherwise around unskinny sturdy) limbs, vaccilated way aimless for his sight.

AS GREGOR SAMSA WOKE FROM AWFUL DREAMS

sonnet

As Gregor Samsa woke from awful dreams
He found himself transformed in his own bed
Into a kind of giant-sized insect.
He lay upon his hardened back to see
In this demented morning reverie
When he could barely stretch to raise his head
His arched, domed, and segmented abdomen
While many legs above flailed helplessly.

"What's happened to me," Gregor had to say.
It was no dream, he came to realize:
His room appeared as any other day
The four walls and cramped space did not surprise.
And there upon the wall he looked at her,
The picture of a lady dressed in fur.

The window drew his gaze and he could hear
The raindrops and their melancholy dirge
If only he'd fall back asleep to purge
This madness that had stricken him to fear
Restrictions now impossibly austere:
No matter how he moved he couldn't surge
To rearrange his body in the urge
To rest as he would usually here.

"Oh God," he said, "what a hard job I've got.
Day after day, to go out on the road,
Enduring lumpy beds and meals of rot,
Acquaintences whose glib banter would corrode!
The hope of lasting friendship to fare well.
Oh, let the devil take it all to hell."

AN ALTERATION

tautogram

As A. awoke after an awful anesthetic accident, A. ascertained an alteration: an awesomely
amplified ant/arachnid assumed A's anatomy.
Aback, an adamant armored accessory agglom-
erated A's ass, and as A's attitude arose aware,
an abdomen appeared apportioned as arched and
adumbrated auburn adobes. Atop, an Afghan almost absconded away; above, A's astonishing
additional appendages addled aimlessly.

"An atrocity! An abortion!" A. announced.
Ain't an abberation. As an act, A.'s adjustment
actualized.

A RARE VEER

left hand liponym

As Greg S reverted after savage z reves
Greg was aware a great trade reared
Greg was a fat badass vast crawdad scarab!

Recast as a crab
Greg saw carved scarred abs
Scattered wee feet
waved a fast raw rage
as fazed Greg gazed

#Egad! fate excavates a grave!#
cadaver Greg averred

AS INSECT GREGOR GIGANTIC

homolexical, from each sentence end to middle

As insect, Gregor gigantic Samsa a) awoke into one bed morning his from in uneasy transformed dreams himself he found. He completely was off lying slide on to his about hard was as, and it, position were in armor-plated keep back hardly, and could when bedspread, he the lifted which his of head top somewhat on, he segments could arched see stiff his into domed divided brown belly. His eyes many his legs, before which helplessly were waved pitifully bulk thin, his in of comparison rest to the.

"What's me happened to?" he say had to. It dream was no. His walls room, familiar a four regular the man's between bedroom quiet, only lay smaller. Above frame, the gilt table pretty, where a collection into of put samples, and was magazine unpacked illustrated, and an out of Samsa out was cut a recently traveling he salesman hung, which the picture. It disappeared showed had a forearm lady, her with of a whole fur the cap which on into and muff a fur, fur huge stole a sitting spectator upright the and to holding out.

Gregor's melancholy eyes quite turned him next made to gutter the window, window and the gray on sky hearing on raindrops beating. How over about himself sleeping turn longer couldn't, and he, forgetting condition all present this, his nonsense in he and wondered side, but right it his couldn't on be sleep done to for accustomed he was. However again much back he his forced onto himself rolled toward always his he right side. He before tried experienced it never at had least hundreds he of ache times, dull shutting faint his some eyes side to his keep in from in seeing feel his to flailing began legs, he and when only stopped.

Oh, have God, I/he/I thought, job an exhausting. Day out in day. It's friends, much become worse never than, and doing new work always in, are the that office acquaintences, and casual; there's meals, the irregular worry, and about bed time-tables. The all devil it take.

THE FORMS A META MISS

spoonerism

As Segor Gramsa awoke nun warming drum un-freezing seams, he found trim self hands formed bin is head into a guy sand dick inject. Lea hay honest bard hack, and when he tiff head his led, he saw a loam dike dab own nym in egg scents where his spread bed whipped a sleigh. A mate granny legs, fit a plea thin, bailed of love him.

Shoaly hit, wee Hun turd. It was drone Nimes. His room, a mourn all red boom smut baller quay lie it twee bean war falls. On the bait all, a low sheck con of pun act sample spray led out. Segor Gramsa was a male son. Wan the all fuzz a tow whoa he had free moved rum a saga mean and put into a frill dead game. It lowed a shady, rare wing furs, hitting to sold doubt to the text baiter a fig burr muff into which fur war harm had piss adheered.

Turning to the din woe, he saw the cry skuzz way rearing drain hops on the gain rutter and he was cussed melon jolly. Nigh watt pee sling a mitt bore and gore fetting this sub turd ditty, he thought, nut bow knee hood cot earn dover on his sight ride where he more nully slept. Tree hide levers all times and whopped sten he fee ban goo teal a feign he hadn't pelt fee bore.

Go hod, rehaled, jut an awe wool fob I have. Aid din, aid doubt. It's thirst wan owing to guffaw this, what with rowing on the goad, gaming train nun sheck Huns, beard weds and mawfull eels, male hello fell wet say fizz who never key bum friends. Who tell with it!

THE METAMOPHOSIS MEETING SOLDIERS OF THE IZMAILOVSKY REGIMENT APRIL 10 (23), 1917

kafka/lenin transplant mash-up

As comrade soldiers awoke the question of the state system one morning from uneasy dreams, we found ourselves transformed into gigantic insect capitalists, in whose hands we were lying on hard, as if armor-plated, state power, and when we desired a parliamentary bourgois republic, we could see our domed, brown belly divided into segments, that is, a state system where there is no tsar, but where the bedspread remains in the hands of the capitalists about to slide off completely to govern the country by means of our many legs of the old institutions, which were pitifully thin compared to the bulk of the police, the bureaucracy, and the standing army flailing helplessly before our eyes.

What happened to us? We desired a different republic. It was no dream; it was more in keeping with the interests of the people. Our room, more democratic, was a regular revolutionary bedroom, only smaller, in which lay workers and soldiers of Petrograd between the familiar walls. Over thrown tsarism above the table on which the cleaned out police from the collection of samples was unpacked from the capital, we were traveling salesmen, the workers of the world, hung with pride and hope, the picture which we had cut out of the revolutionary soldiers of Russia as the vanguard of an illustrated magazine, and put into a pretty gilt frame. It showed a lady of the world's liberating army of the working class dressed in fur, sitting upright, and holding out to the revolution a huge fur muff which, once begun, had to be strengthened. Her forearm had disappeared and carried on.

Our eyes turned to not allow the police to be the window, and the gray sky to be re-established raindrops beating on the window gutter. All power to the state made us melancholy. From the bottom up, how about sleeping a bit longer from the remotest little village, and forgetting this nonsense to every street block of Petrograd? we thought. But it could not be done to the Soviets of Workers, Soldiers, Agricultural Laborers, for we were accustomed to sleeping with Peasants and other Deputies. On our right side in our present condition, the central state of power uniting us could not turn itself over. However violently, these local Soviets tried a hundred times, shutting their eyes to keep from seeing the Constituent Assembly, and only stopped when we began to feel a National Assembly or Council of Soviets or whatever pain we had never felt before.

Oh God, we thought, not the police, not the bureaucracy, who are unanswerable to what an awful job we have: traveling day in, day out to the people, and placed above the people. It's worse than the standing army at the office, separated from the people constantly on the road, but the people themselves, universally armed and united in bed and irregular meals, Soviets, casual acquaintances that are never friends, must run the state. It is the devil who will establish the necessary order, take it all.

AS HE

split sentences re-combined

As Gregor Samsa awoke one morning from uneasy dreams, he waved helplessly before his eyes. His many legs, pitifully thin in comparison to his body, could hardly keep from sliding off completely. Transformed into a giant insect, he was lying on his hard, as if armor-plated, back.

He lifted his head and could see his domed belly divided into no dream. A huge muff where her forearm had disappeared, a regular man's bedroom, only smaller, between four familiar walls, showed a lady, sitting upright and holding out above the table where a sample case was unpacked and spread out. Put into a pretty gilt frame, Samsa was a traveling salesman.

His gaze turned to the window when he felt a dull ache he had never felt before. He tried a hundred times, shutting his eyes to keep from seeing the overcast sky, the raindrops beating. Violently he forced himself, made him quite melancholy. He always rolled onto his back again about sleeping a little more and forgetting all this nonsense.

Oh, God, take it all. The devil awful job I have. Never become friends day after day. It's worse than the bed and meals, the casual acquaintances. Worrying about train connections doing regular work at the office, there's the constant travel.

FROM UNEASY DREAMS

prepositional phrases

From uneasy dreams in his bed into a gigantic insect on his hard back when he lifted into stiff arched segments on top of which in position about to slide off completely to the rest of him before his eyes.

To me between four walls above the table on which a sample case out of a magazine into a pretty gilt frame with a fur cap out to the spectator into which her forearm disappeared.

To the window on the window on his right side in his present condition toward his right side onto his back at least in his side.

After day in the office on top of that of constant travel of worrying about train time-tables.

AS THE HELL WITH IT

run-on

as Gregor Samsa awoke one morning from uneasy dreams he found himself transformed into a gigantic insect on his hard as if armor-plated back and when he lifted his head he could see his domed brown belly divided into stiff arched segments the bedspread could hardly stay on his many pitifully thin legs flailing helplessly happened to me what was no dream his regular bedroom only smaller lay quiet between familiar walls above the table where a sample case lay unpacked and spread out he was a salesman hung a picture he'd cut out of a magazine and put in a pretty frame a lady in furs sitting upright and holding out a huge fur muff where her forearm had disappeared his gaze turning to the window and the gray sky raindrops beating on the gutter made him quite melancholy about sleeping a bit more and forgetting all this nonsense but he couldn't since he was used to sleeping on his right side and he couldn't turn over tried a hundred times shutting his eyes to keep from seeing his legs and only stopped when he began to feel a dull pain he'd never felt before God what an awful job I have he thought traveling day after day worse than going to the office there's the trouble of constantly being on the road of worrying about train connections and beds and meals and casual acquaintances who never become real friends the hell with it

IT ALL

endings

a gigantic insect about to slide off completely
    flailing before his eyes

to me no dream familiar walls gilt frame had dis-
    appeared

melancholy couldn't turn over on his back felt
    before

job I have after day never friends it all

AFTER KAFKA AFTERWORD

Ever since a college literature course permitted me to turn in parodies rather than papers on the novelists we studied, I've been drawn to revising the works of other writers. This differs from the conceptual writing practice of reproducing works word for word, as Simon Morris did when he retyped *On the Road* in a blog and published it, page by page from last page to first, as *Getting Inside Jack Kerouac's Head* (Information as Material, 2010). I'm more manipulative. I translated *On the Road* into business jargon and rearranged the scenes to write a corporate history/novel, *On the Roast* (Chiasmus, 2004), wrote *The Waste Land* backwards; and, to test the limits of various constraints, I've rendered passages from *The Odyssey*, *Exercises in Style*, the Bible, and other works into whatever constraint drove the book I was writing. A recent turn toward anagrams sent me to Franz Kafka (1883–1924).

Since K. Silem Mohammad brilliantly spun Shakespeare's sonnets into *The Sonnagrams* (Slack Buddha, 2009), I figured that any new commitment to anagrams must deal with a work that addressed the topic of transformation: either *Metamorphoses* or *The Metamorphosis*. Ovid's epic seemed too long (and perhaps too unfamiliar) for such an extreme constraint, while Kafka's compact and renowned novella offered the potential to support whatever mangling I had in mind.

Although a work in translation poses an additional problem to those who are most intent on making sense of the work (and, who are perhaps not as concerned with other patterns that help make the original text what it is), this problem suits the topic of transformation. I began with translations by Willa and Edwin Muir (*Franz Kafka: The Complete Stories*, Shocken Books, 1946), Stanley Applebaum (*The Metamorphosis and Other Stories*, Dover Thrift Editions, 1995), and Stanley Corngold (*The Metamorphosis*, Bantam, 1972), and revised them to make them more adaptable to an English-to-English anagram translation.

I was also intrigued by German-to-English anagram translation, the wrangling of so many high-point Scrabble letters, and the approach this provided to the text. This approach more emphasizes the patterns of language that are not primarily concerned with semantic sense. I yearned to apply a series of Oulipian translation techniques and constraints to Kafka's opening paragraphs, but first I had to get into the flow of the story and transform it, to retain the narration and supplement it with the anagram version rather than to produce an all-anagram version.

A fundamental challenge of standard semantic translation comes out in the first iconic sentence: interpretations vary. Without going to the wonderful lengths Caroline Bergvall does when she reproduces 48 different renderings of the beginning of *The Divine Comedy* in her poem *VIA*, Stanley Corngold supplies a section of explanatory notes on terms that is almost as long as the text. Two pages discuss "ungeheuren Ungeziefer." One translator's "gigantic insect" is another's "monstrous vermin," with variations bearing on making the thing more or less identifiable. Later in the story, a character may refer to it/him as a "dung beetle" a "blood-sucking vermin" or a "cockroach," all of which contribute to an impression that Corngold seems to prefer to leave incomplete in the opening. As for the monstrous vermin who would suck the blood out of Kafka's masterwork by riddling it with anagrams, these notes constitute an open interpretation invitation.

Decades after first encountering *The Metamorphosis*, I threw myself back into the complexity of Kafka's prose. Sentences tend to be longer than the opening lines, as they explore a nuanced range of reactions to the extraordinary events and circumstances the characters experience. Parenthetical digressions lend themselves well to the procedural maniac bent on larding the lines with modifications. Paragraphs can go on for pages, sometimes containing dialogues that conventional usage would break into separate paragraphs, as if these dialogues are supposed to be occurring simultaneously in the narrative and/or in the mind of a character. Although some characters are stock figures, the principals of the story have intriguing backgrounds and prospects. The very idea of a family being supported by a son who lives with them while holding a job he hates may seem unusual (if all too familiar to Kafka himself), and to have this son spend night after night at home doing needlepoint while his father dozes off, mother directs the servant, and sister dreams of a future in the music conservatory is only somewhat less bizarre than having the son wake up one day as a big bug. The unreasonably measured and understandably hysterical reactions of people to the new Gregor moderate the proceedings, and the consequences of the father going to work as a bank messenger and the family taking in a trio of haughty lodgers to make ends meet seem right at home. And we really know we're in another world when an office manager comes to the flat just because Gregor was missing from work.

Absurdities and all, there is something affecting about the plight of the Samsa family as they cope with Gregor's condition, especially as Gregor, despite everything, loves his parents and sister and wishes not to inflict hardship on them, even as he may resent how they treat him. His death is somber, then played for laughs, and finally accepted.

In light of the many writers whose work is routinely branded by reviewers as "Kafkaesque," as well as more direct, thorough, and developed appreciations, such as Lance Olsen's *Anxious Pleasures: A Novel After Kafka* (Shoemaker and Hoard, 2007), which imagines the inner lives of the Samsas, I wonder where my project belongs.

Maybe the appeal of venturing into a maze of translations and other constraints is analogous to the appeal a traveling salesman living with his parents and sister at the turn of the last century might have felt when, at the end of another awful day of work, he took up his needles to play.

Doug Nufer's novels include *Lifeline Rule* (Spuyten Duyvil, 2015), *By Kelman Out of Pessoa* (Les Figues, 2011), *The Mudflat Man/The River Boys* (soultheft records, 2006), *On the Roast* (Chiasmus, 2004), *Negativeland* (Autonomedia, 2004), and *Never Again* (Black Square, 2004). He is the author of the poetry collections *The Me Theme* (Sagging Meniscus, 2017), *We Were Werewolves* (Make Now, 2008), *The Dammed* (ubu.com, 2011), and *Lounge Acts* (Insert Blanc, 2013). He sells wine in Seattle.

Photo by Peggy Sullivan.